Out Of Bounds

Pure Escapes

Kit Kyndall

Published by Amourisa Press, 2021.

Blurb

AS MY SISTER'S BEST friend and barely out of college, she's totally out of bounds...

Evan

I volunteer to let my sister's best friend stay with me for a few weeks when she moves to Manhattan. I remember her as an awkward teenager, but she's all grown up—though still twelve years younger than me. I shouldn't want her, but I can't help it. I dream about touching her, and I don't know how long my tenuous control will last. My meddling business partner keeps warning me not to get involved to preserve my image, so my desire must be transparent. If Vanessa can see it, so will my family. I don't want anything to come between us, but how can I give up Keaton?

Keaton

I thought my silly crush on Evan had faded away, but it's roaring back to life the more time I spend with him. I'm afraid it's not just a crush this time. As we get emotionally—and physically—closer, my feelings deepen. I think his do as well, but we know this can't last. His family, who is practically like mine as well, will never approve. I know my best friend will hate me if she finds out. How can there be a happy ending for us with so many obstacles in our way?

Chapter One

Evan

WHEN I VOLUNTEERED to let Keaton stay with me for the first few weeks after her move to New York City, I had done it out of kindness and the familial connection. After all, she's my sister's best friend and has been since kindergarten, and she's lived with my parents ever since she was fourteen, when her own were killed in a car accident.

I hadn't given it much thought either way, and I hadn't known what to expect, but now as I open the door after the doorbell rings, my mouth becomes dry, and I have the urge to wipe my hands down my jeans as my palms moisten. "Keaton?" I know it's her. I mean, it has to be, but she sure looks different from the last time I remember seeing her. I haven't been home much for the last several years, and I've skipped three of the last four Christmases with being too busy with my life in Manhattan. She would've been nineteen the last time I saw her, and she'd still been kind of chubby and awkward then.

As I look at her now, it's obvious all the baby fat is gone. Instead, even with the horrible sweats and T-shirt she wears, I just see a desirable woman—not just one who's twelve years younger than me and should be like a sister. To be fair, I had already been away from home when she moved in with my folks and Meghan.

She blinks at me, looking confused. "Of course. You are expecting me, aren't you?" She nibbles on her lower lip for a minute, looking anxious. "I was afraid this was a bad idea. I told Meghan you wouldn't want me in your way, ruining your hookups and whatever. I can just get a hotel..."

Before she can turn and walk away, I gently grasp her wrist and pull her inside. "Of course, I was expecting you. I just haven't seen you for a few years. You've changed." It's strange how different she really looks. She still wears no makeup, her hair is in a messy bun, and those clothes do her no favor, but at some point, she'd outgrown the awkward teenage phase to become a lovely young woman.

I might not have even noticed if I'd seen her regularly over the last three years, because it was the kind of quiet beauty that developed over time. I was able to see the contrast now since I hadn't seen her, and it forms a lump in my throat. I cough to clear it as I lead her around the apartment. "Let me give you the tour."

I take her through the rooms, saving the living room almost for last, aside from her bedroom. I'm sure she's going to appreciate the view, and I hold my breath with anticipation for a moment as she stands in front of the wall that's almost entirely dominated by windows and glances out at the city below.

Her lips part in a gasp, and her cheeks bloom with color as she surveys the city spread out before her. There's a sparkle in her blue eyes, and when she turns to look at me, she's clearly enthralled. "I had no idea you have such an amazing view."

I shrug a shoulder. "It's the reason I bought this place." I don't bother telling her I was on a list for almost a year, waiting for an opening in the luxurious, exclusive Beaumont Building.

She looks impressed, and after her awkward comment about me hooking up and her blocking such abilities, I half-expect her to blurt out a gauche comment about the expense, but she says nothing. I realize the silence has lengthened between us, and it threatens to become uncomfortable, so I run a hand through my short dark hair and clear my throat. "Let me show you your room."

"Just your guestroom. I wouldn't presume to call it my room." She seems perfectly serious.

I don't bother to argue with her, for what's the point? This is supposed to be temporary, but I already dislike the idea of her moving out. I try not to analyze why that might be, and she follows closely enough behind me that I can smell her enticing aroma. Cinnamon and vanilla, and it's overlaid with a different scent that seems entirely her own.

When I reach the doorway and step back so she can pass by me, her body brushes against mine, and I get a good whiff of her hair. It has that same enticing cinnamon/vanilla scent, and I want to bury my face in it. Of course, I have more self-control than to do something so crazy. Instead, I move and strive for an aloof expression. "I'll leave you to settle in, and when you're ready, we can order in takeout."

She nods her agreement as she sets her duffle bag on the bed. I realize I should've offered to take it for her, but I had been temporarily stunned by the realization Keaton is all grown up. I close the door behind me as I walk away, going to the living room and standing in front of the windows. Though I paid an exorbitant amount for this view, I'm not really seeing the city before me right now.

Instead, I contrast the image of the young girl I remember with the woman she has become, and I feel a little anxiety about having her in my place. I tell myself I'd never do anything inappropriate, reminding myself she's twelve years younger and certainly naïve, particularly when it comes to the lifestyle I lead. Our small Michigan town can't possibly have prepared her for life in the big city. I recall how bewildering and overwhelming it felt to me when I first arrived eleven years ago, and I know she's in no place to deal with anything like me panting after her. She'd probably be confused and maybe even disgusted by the old guy.

That thought is enough to bring me in line, and when she comes into the room a short time later, I manage to control myself even when I realize her hair is now down around her face and falling along her back instead of confined to the messy bun. I have a difficult time looking away for a moment, but she doesn't seem to realize I'm staring.

Instead, she walks closer to me, slipping her hands into the pockets of her sweats as she stands in front of me and rocks back and forth lightly on her feet. 'You mentioned takeout?" As she speaks, her stomach rumbles, and she blushes. "Sorry, but I couldn't handle the airline food, and my one layover was hours ago."

I nod in understanding, briefly wondering if I should've offered to meet her at the airport. It hadn't even occurred to me until now, and I realize how thoughtless it was to just give her the address and expect her to find her way to my apartment. That she clearly handled it doesn't mitigate the discomfort I feel for the oversight, and I briefly remember the lessons my dad and mom always gave me about manners. Has living in Manhattan changed me so much that I've forgotten the basic courtesies?

I turn away from her, unsettled by my thoughts, and open a drawer to pull out various takeout menus. I have most of them memorized, because I have little time to cook with my business commitments, but I'm sure she'll want to peruse them all. The maid service hasn't touched them, and I'm grateful for that.

She sits down at the kitchen table nearby, spreading them before her. I grin as I see her unbridled enthusiasm. If I remember correctly, Keaton always did appreciate a wide variety of food, and she liked to try everything new. I know for sure there are options among the menus that she was unlikely to ever try in Michigan, unless maybe she visited one of the larger cities.

Ultimately, she selects one of my favorite places, a little Asian restaurant that has a mashup of Filipino, Malaysian, and Thai cuisine. My eyes widened slightly when she picks the number seventeen, which is my usual. I nod and pull up the restaurant in my contacts, quickly placing the order. I recognize the voice of the owner when she answers, and clearly, Soo recognizes me as well. "Good evening, Mr. Middleton. Will you have your usual?"

"Yeah, but two of them."

"You must be very hungry." She laughs as she takes my order and hangs up a few minutes later.

We just have to kill some time until the food arrives, and though I gave her a basic tour of the kitchen earlier, I spend the next few minutes showing her how the fridge is organized, and where she can find the good wine.

"I don't think I know anything about good wine." She laughs as she shares that. "I just finished college. I'm still in the *Arbor Mist* phase of life."

I smile in amusement, though it's an uncomfortable reminder of just how different we are, and how far apart in our stages of life. I select a rosé, remove the cork, and fill two glasses for us. "You have to let me know if this can compare to *Arbor Mist*."

She takes the glass and sips lightly, and her eyes widen with surprise. "I have to admit, this is way better than the screw-top stuff I usually drink."

I don't bother to tell her she can buy ten bottles of her cheap crap for the price of this one, just enjoying her obvious pleasure in the vintage. It's a reminder she still has plenty of time to learn anything she might want to know. It's not like she's a baby, who has to be protected.

Except maybe from me. I reach that conclusion when she jumps to her feet as the doorbell rings a short time later, and I catch an enticing glimpse of the jiggle of her breasts as she bounces to the door. She answers, paying before I have a chance to tell her I have a tab with the restaurant. I'm hovering nearby when she closes the door and hands me one of the boxes as she takes the other. She heads to the kitchen, and I follow behind her, going to the cabinet to remove plates. She looks at me askance as she pops open a Styrofoam container. "You're going to use plates?"

Unexpectedly, I feel judged. "I don't like eating out of Styrofoam." I could mention I have a cleaning service that will deal with the dishes, but I don't think that will convince her to see things my way.

After a second, she shrugs. "Your house, your rules."

I almost drop the plates as her words inspire thoughts they definitely shouldn't—the kind involving me telling her what to do, and her instantly obeying.

Clearing my throat once more, afraid she's going to think I have a cold with all the times I've had to do it so far, I turn to her and hold out a plate. She takes it and dumps her food almost indiscriminately on the plate.

I'm more methodical, taking time to separate into neat piles. I dislike food touching, and she seems vaguely amused when she sees my plate as I lift it, along with a glass of wine, and suggest, "Why don't we eat in the living room?"

When she nods her agreement, the neck of her oversized T-shirt slides down slightly, revealing her bra strap. It's just a basic white, and I'm certain it's the chain store kind that offers nothing special, but my mouth is still suddenly dry, and my fingers twitch as I think about tugging down the T-shirt to reveal more. Of course, I restrain myself and allow her to precede me. My gaze does drop to her rounded butt to appreciate the view. I'm not an animal, but I'm sure as hell not a saint either.

We settle in front of the TV, and I offer her the remote. She selects a comedy show I grew up watching, and I arch a brow. "I'm surprised you like this."

"I really like the classics."

Ouch. I wince at that and turn my attention to the food. I discreetly observe her use chopsticks, and she impresses me with their mastery. Of course, Chinese food is common in Michigan, so I shouldn't be surprised that she knows how to use them. I fear Manhattan has made me a bit of a snob.

At first, we focus on eating, but as she works her way through the food, she starts to talk, clearly more sated now. "I really can't thank you enough for this, Evan. I know what an imposition it is, and I promise I won't be in your hair for long. I've been looking for an apartment for weeks, ever since I got the job with Star Gaming, but everything is so expensive, or it requires taking a billion subway rides... I don't know if this is going to work out, but I feel like I have to try."

I frown at her. "You can make it work. I was in a similar position when I first arrived, if you recall?"

She nods tentatively. "Things were a little different though. You were an early graduate with an MBA and impressive possibilities ahead of you."

I arch a brow. "That sounds like a textbook quote from Mom."

"Lily might've said that a few times," says Keaton with a grin.

I shrug, feeling uncomfortable with the discussion, since it makes me sound like some prodigy. I was never that. I was just eager to escape our small town and see more of the world, so I worked hard to graduate early and excelled. "I was on the fast track, but you've no doubt heard I got tired of working for other people and walked away. I started my own business, as much as it pained my mother and father."

She frowns, looking defensive. "I don't think Lily and Everett were ever upset that you left your corporate job. They were just worried about you."

I put up a hand. "I agree, but my point is, even with all my so-called advantages, I still had to do things my own way. If I remember anything about you, it's that you can be kind of stubborn."

Her mouth drops open at the accusation, but then she shrugs and laughs. "Yeah, I suppose that's fair."

"With your tenacity, you're going to make this work."

She still looks apprehensive. "I've always wanted to work for Star Gaming. They put out some of the best, and to get hired right out of college is pretty amazing, though I know I'll be doing a lot of the grunt work. I guess I'm just nervous about meeting their expectations."

"I don't think you can fail." I genuinely believe that as I say it. It's true I don't know Keaton as well as I used to, but I definitely remember how she was always one to accomplish her goals and not give up until she did.

She licks her lips before sipping wine. "Even if it doesn't work out here, at least I can say I tried."

I nod my agreement at that, and we finish our meal before settling back on the couch. The sitcom is still on in the background, but we spend the next hour talking about everything and nothing. I'm surprised to discover we have more in common than I expect, but I'm kind of clueless about some of the things she talks about. I've never been much of a gamer, while I remember she and Meghan were always into it from the time they became friends.

"It's an aspect I really enjoy, so I'm trying to incorporate it into my own game."

I've kind of been tuning out the mechanics of the game she's discussing, but that catches my attention. "Your game?"

She looks a little shy as she nods. "I've been designing one on the side. It started out as a project for a class, but after I did one level, I thought it had a lot of potential. I kept going, and I hope to finish it someday in the near future."

I'm impressed. "I thought it took teams of people to design games."

She shrugs her shoulder. "It can, and if I had teams, I wouldn't have spent the last two years working on it myself. I think it'll be done in another twenty levels or so though. I might even put it up for sale." She seems a little daunted by the prospect.

"I'm sure you'll be successful."

She tilts her head and looks at me. "You're different than I remember, Evan."

I shift slightly in my seat, not sure that's a good thing. "How do you mean?"

"You were always busy and self-absorbed." She blushes as she says that. "I'm sorry. Maybe I'm a little too blunt sometimes. I just remember you being involved in your own world. There's nothing wrong with that, but you never really had time for me or Meghan. Now, I can't help feeling like you're my own personal cheerleader."

I blink as I stare at her, not sure how to respond to that. I've been simultaneously insulted and complimented, and all she's done is tell the truth. I've always been more focused on me than others, and even being aware of that trait, it is still uncomfortable when someone else calls it out. Especially when she's twelve years my junior and my little sister's best friend.

She's clearly surprised I'm taking an interest in her and encouraging her. Truthfully, I'm surprised myself, but I'm not about to tell her that. I don't want her to think my motives are murky, and I don't want to believe that either. Just because I feel a level of interest in her I didn't expect to doesn't mean I'm just telling her what she wants to hear. "People change."

She nods, and her gaze is full of appreciation as it sweeps over me. "You have in a lot of ways, but you're still as handsome as I remember." She seems completely clueless about the inappropriateness of her comment. "I told Meghan you were going to hate having me here, because I'd stifle the parade. I just want to let you know that I don't expect you to change anything just because I'm here. I can stay in my room or whatever, and I won't get in the way of you and your *friends*." She gives special significance to the pronunciation of friends.

I frown, feeling a little confused, and also a sting of outrage as I suspect I know what she means. "Can you clarify please?"

She frowns, apparently recognizing there's some displeasure in my tone. "I didn't mean to make things awkward. I just wanted to state upfront that I don't expect you to act like a monk or something while I'm here. This is your place, and I'll stay out of your way any time you want to bring home your women."

I scowl. "Just how many women do you think I'm juggling, Keaton?"

She opens her mouth, but she doesn't speak for a long moment. She starts to blush as she looks away. "I don't know, but probably a lot."

I lean forward to put my empty wine glass on a coaster. "What have I ever done to give you the impression I'm a glorified man-whore?"

She giggles, but she still seems a little ill-at-ease. "It's just some stuff we've heard over the years. Things Meghan heard from Becket, I guess."

I frown at the mention of my best friend. He lives across the country now, so we haven't maintained as much contact as we did for the last few years, but we used to be inseparable. I blush as I realize he's seen the worst of me, particularly my wild phase during college and graduate school, which was difficult to maintain while focusing on graduating early, but I somehow excelled at education *and* sex during that phase of my life.

I can well imagine the things he might've relayed to Meghan, though I'm dismayed that he would do so. I didn't even know he and Meghan were really friends, since he's twelve years older than her. I start to feel a spark of outrage, wondering if my friend has behaved inappropriately with my sister, when it smacks me in the face what a hypocrite I'm being. I'm sitting beside my sister's best friend, who is twelve years younger than me, and as much as I'd like to pretend it's not true, I'm attracted to her. I should be wanting to kick my own ass right about now.

Instead, I struggle to put more distance between us, both physically and emotionally. I lean back and say, "As you said, people change. That phase was a long time ago. Running my own business keeps me pretty busy. About the only woman I see regularly is my partner, Vanessa, and we're focused on business. If that situation changes, I'll keep in mind that you plan to stay out of my way, but I assure you, it's not never-ending orgy time in my apartment."

Even though she's blushing, she starts to laugh. "I guess I'm relieved to hear that. It might be difficult to pick my way through all the bodies scattered across the living room every morning otherwise."

My lips twitch in spite of myself. "We certainly wouldn't want you to be late for work."

"I guess I made a mess out of all of this, but I was just trying to illustrate that I didn't want you to change anything because I'm here. I don't expect you to entertain me or switch your life around to accommodate me while I'm staying with you."

I nod my agreement, and we continue to watch TV for a while until she begins to yawn. It's early by Manhattan standards, but she spent the day traveling, and she looks worn out. As a gentle command, I say, "Get to bed. You look like you need a good night's sleep before you start work in the morning."

She stifles a yawn, not bothering to argue as she stands up. "I guess it's been a long day, and wine always makes me sleepy. Thanks again for everything, Evan."

I nod at her and watch her walk away. As she disappears down the hall, I recall her assurance that she doesn't want my life to change just because she's here. I fear it's already too late, and I realize I could be in trouble.

Chapter Two

Keaton

I MANAGE TO FIND THE energy to take a shower before collapsing into the bed. It's sinfully comfortable, but I'm not surprised by that. The level of luxury in this apartment would've made me more surprised if it had been a hard lump. It's clear Evan has done all right for himself, and he certainly seems different from the driven, self-absorbed boy and young man I remember.

One thing hasn't changed—he's just as hot as ever. I sigh in disgust at myself, having hoped I had finally buried the remnants of the crush I've had for him for years. That had been part of my hesitation at accepting this arrangement when Meghan made the suggestion and set it all up with Evan.

The last thing I want to do is make a fool of myself or reveal I've had a thing for him for years. I really thought I had moved past all this, and after spending a year dating a guy back home before breaking things off to move to New York, it's not like I've been inexperienced with relationships. I'm certainly old enough to control a response and also recognize it's all physical.

There's definitely a difference though. The crush I had before was all physical, and certainly not inspired by any of his personality traits. He seems different now. Kinder, more approachable, and actually personally interested in me. Not in a romantic way, I hasten to remind myself before torturing myself with memories of some of the idiotic things I said this evening.

I've always been a little too quick to speak my mind without always thinking things through, and tonight has proven no exception. I'd planned to conduct myself with dignity and quiet grace, but those traits just aren't me. I'll have to be on my guard around him lest I blurt out something ridiculous and embarrassing. I thought I had been, and I still managed to say stupid things.

I shake my head at myself as I turn over in bed, curling into a ball and snuggling under the covers. The apartment maintains perfect temperature, but I had taken time to turn down the thermostat in my room before getting into bed. It's pleasantly cold in here now, and the comforter is warmer than I expected, considering how light it is. That probably means it cost more than my first month's salary, and I try not to think about that. It will leave me feeling inadequate at minimum.

Resolving to better control my tongue and think before I spoke in future, I drift off to sleep. I wake before my alarm the next morning, due to a combination of anxiety, excitement, and having slept like the dead for many hours.

After getting ready, I enter the kitchen and find a few staples in the fridge. Since Evan doesn't really cook, I decide to make him breakfast as a thank you for everything he's done so far. He doesn't have anything to make extravagant pancakes, like chocolate chips or pumpkin or bananas, but I can make a serviceable version, along with eggs and bacon.

I hear him stirring behind me in the doorway just as I turn with his plate and place it on the table. It's a near thing, and it lands with a slight clatter. I nearly lost my grip on it at my first sight of him in a three-piece suit. I imagine I've seen him dress similarly in the past, but I never really noticed before how amazing he looks clad so elegantly. I clear my throat and gesture to the fridge. "Would you like orange juice?"

He shakes his head. "Coffee'll do." As he speaks, he slips a pod into the lavish coffeemaker. It has so many bells and whistles I was afraid to look at it earlier, let alone try to navigate making coffee. I watch discreetly now as he makes a simple cup before following suit. At least now I can brew coffee, but I'm sure this thing is state-of-the-art. It can probably make cappuccinos, espresso, and possibly book a flight to Mars.

I put my plate on the table and sit down across from him, trying to be careful about what I say.

He frowns after a few minutes. "Did you rest well?"

I nod as I finish a bite of pancakes. "That has to be the best bed ever."

"You're not much of a morning person then?"

I tilt my head slightly. "I don't think that's me. Meghan always complains I'm disgustingly cheerful in the morning."

He frowns. "You just don't seem very cheerful or upbeat right now. Are you nervous?"

I almost blow it by revealing how nervous I am about saying something stupid, but then I realize he must be talking about my new job. That causes a rush of anxiety as well, and my stomach clenches as I nod. "Yeah, I'm pretty nervous."

He reaches across the table and squeezes my hand. It's a brief, casual gesture that means nothing, so why can I still feel my skin tingling even minutes later?

He says, "You'll do just fine. They're going to love you." His hand returns to his lap, and he finishes breakfast.

I struggle to do the same, though my appetite has fled. Having to watch everything I say is somewhat exhausting, and combined with the worry I won't be able to meet the demands my new job, ensures I won't be finishing the rest of my breakfast. I push it away after a second and focus on the coffee instead.

It's delicious, with a hint of chocolate and cherry. It's smooth, and there's no bitterness when I swallow despite its lack of cream or sugar. It's probably some exotic variety grown in the shade of Kilimanjaro before being harvested by hand, and I appreciate how wonderful it is, though I know I'll never be able to afford it.

He leaves a few minutes later, and I do the same. "Can I give you a lift?" he asks in the elevator on the way down.

My eyes widen. "You have a car in Manhattan?" It seems kind of crazy to me from everything I've researched.

He shakes his head. "No... Yes, kind of. I hire a car service to pick me up to take me to work and bring me home each day. I'm sure the driver can take you wherever you're headed to as well."

When I tell him the address of Star Gaming, he winces. "I'm afraid that's the other direction from where I'm going, but it's only about eight blocks from here. Do you feel comfortable getting to your job?"

"I'm going to treat myself to a taxi today." It's a walkable distance to and from work, but I probably can't walk everywhere I want to go in New York City. I know I have to figure out public transportation, but I don't want to mess with that on my first day.

We linger together in the foyer for a moment after stepping out of the elevator. It seems like he wants to say something else, but he finally just nods. "Good luck today."

"Thanks." I watch him walk away, appreciating the fine form he presents doing so. With his firm body, dark brown locks, and sparkling blue eyes, it's no wonder I've lusted after him all these years, but I never really liked him before. I mean, I put up with him, but he was always older, aloof, and seemingly full of himself.

So far, he's showed a different side of himself, and I worry it's only going to fuel the crush I feel. I can't let that happen, because I don't want to be the pathetic joke who falls in love with my best friend's brother. He's completely unattainable, and at twelve years older than me, with a ton more life experience, there's no way he's ever going to look twice at me. I don't want to be the fool, so I set aside everything I'm feeling for him, telling myself it's all in my head, and flag down a taxi.

I RETURN TO THE APARTMENT that evening feeling despondent. My first day was kind of a disaster, and I'm really second-guessing my choice to move here so far away from everything I know with Evan as my only tentative ally. He mentioned working long hours, so I'm surprised to find he's home when I open the door and step inside. I can smell spices in the air that remind me of Mexico, so I'm not surprised to find an assortment of Mexican takeout arranged on the kitchen table when I enter moments later.

I unbutton my jacket and toss it across the back of the chair I plan to sit in, relieved to have that confinement lifted. It's another relief to kick off my heels. They're short and sensible, since I never learned how to wear anything else, but they're still uncomfortable. I'd gladly claw off my pantyhose and rip them into shreds with my nonexistent fingernails, but Evan's presence has a prohibitive effect on that.

He turns to me, holding out a plate. "How was...?" He trails off a frown. "You look rough."

I manage a small smile. "It was a rough day. I felt like I was constantly behind, and I don't think I learned anything of value from my classes, at least when it applies to Star Gaming. My boss, Bill Smith, clearly dislikes me already. Plus, he's kinda creepy."

He scowls. "Creepy in what way?"

"I don't know." I shrug a shoulder as I start to serve myself enchiladas. "He just likes to stand too close. He has this way of looming around, like he's trying to intimidate you. I don't know. It just didn't feel right."

He clearly doesn't like that. "You have to watch out for him."

I blink as I infer his meaning. "Oh, I don't think I'm in any true danger of being harassed. He's just kind of old and creepy."

He frowns. "How old is he?"

I shrug. "Maybe forty."

He winces then, and he quickly looks away.

I pick at the enchiladas for a moment, not sure how to tell him Mexican is my least favorite cuisine. I take a bite, and it's all I can do not to grimace. It has cilantro in it. It's the most disgusting spice ever, except for maybe fennel.

"You don't like Mexican." He says it like a statement of fact.

I look up at him, smiling. "It's fine."

He laughs as he shakes his head. "No, it's not. I just remembered Mom telling me how you all went to Mexico a few summers ago, and you had to find every American hamburger joint you could track down. If I recall, you spent a lot of that week going hungry."

I shrug sheepishly. "I was kind of a spoiled brat. Seriously, this is fine." I struggle to hide a frown as the taste of cilantro lingers on my tongue, like bitter soap. How can people stand to eat this?

"You know what? I can just take this for lunch tomorrow. Let's go out for dinner."

I frown at him. "Really, you don't have to go to all that trouble. I can make do with this just fine." I can always eat the rice and beans. They're the most palatable options available...unless they have cilantro too.

He shakes his head. "Believe it or not, I was actually trying to do something nice. I remembered you guys going to Mexico, and Mom said you had loved it. I assumed that extended to the cuisine."

I shrug a shoulder. "The history and culture are amazing, but the food isn't my favorite." I might as well be honest. He already knows, doesn't he?

"So, dinner out it is. What would you rather have?"

I hesitate. "I really don't want to put you out."

"I'm taking you out, so pick a place." He sounds slightly inflexible, and he gives me a stern look.

Part of me wants to protest the heavy-handed manner, but another part of me can't deny how damp my panties get from the tone of voice and the look he gives me. I clear my throat and say, "Italian?" I ask it more like a question than a suggestion.

"Italian it is." He looks at my attire. "Do you want to change into something more casual?"

Boy, do I ever. I nod eagerly and get up, scooping up my shoes off the floor and grabbing my jacket to rush down the hallway to the guestroom.

I'd like to choose something like jeans and a hoodie, but I have a feeling even casual Italian is something fancier than I'm used to with Evan, so I select a floral dress instead. It's still loose and comfortable, but it should be appropriate for anywhere he wants to take me.

Just thinking about Evan taking me—and certainly not to a restaurant—makes me lean against the wall and fan my face with my hand for a moment before I shove my feet into flats and rejoin him.

He's taken advantage of the opportunity and changed out of his vest and shirt, though he'd already shed the tie and jacket before I'd arrived at the apartment. He's wearing khakis and a polo now, and he seems more approachable. When he holds out his arm, I slip mine through without thought, telling myself it's just a friendly gesture as we take the elevator down a few moments later.

Chapter Three

I TAKE KEATON TO MY favorite Italian restaurant, which is only a few blocks away from the apartment and a quick walk. The host knows me when I enter, and he beams. It's good to see you again, Mr. Middleton."

"You as well, Giovanni." I shake his hand before he leads us to a table by the window. This is a good place for people-watching, and it's my usual table. When Giovanni assists Keaton into her seat, I feel a little put out, since I'd planned to do that.

I wait until the sommelier has poured wine, and our first courses are ordered before leaning closer to say, "Tell me more about your creepy boss."

Keaton looks dismayed. "Like I said, it's probably nothing. Maybe I'm just projecting, since it's obvious he's unhappy with my work and skill levels."

I frown, fighting back a surge of jealousy I have no right to feel, along with a wave of anger directed solely at her boss. "If he doesn't like your skillset, why did he hire you?"

She sips the red wine before answering. "That wasn't Mr. Smith's decision. I was hired by a committee via HR procedures. One of my new coworkers told me Mr. Smith wanted to hire his nephew for the job, so it's probably the reason he's treating me like I don't know what I'm doing." She looks down, nibbling on her lip. "I'll admit, there were some things I wasn't expecting and hadn't learned."

"I'm sure you'll pick it up quickly. Let me know if he continues to be a problem."

She tilts her head slightly and arches a brow at me. "How are you going to help? You're not his boss, you're not an attorney, and you're certainly not my babysitter. I can handle it myself, Evan." She sounds confident and reasonable as she says the words.

I still have the instinctive urge to protest, to insist I can step in and bring Bill Smith back into line, but I still the impulse. Even if I were more than Keaton's friend and roommate, I have no right to step in with her boss. It's true there's probably nothing official I can do to get him to back down, but if he continues his mistreatment of her, he'll be talking to me whether Keaton likes it or not.

Our pasta arrives then, and we dig in. We're about halfway through our meal when I hear the click of heels on the tile floor as a woman approaches us. I quickly recognize Vanessa, my business partner, and smile at her as I get to my feet. "What are you doing here?"

Without waiting, she takes a seat, and I return to my chair, since she clearly doesn't want me to help her with hers. "I was walking by and saw you in the window." Her gaze moves to Keaton, and I see her grimace. "Who's your young little date?"

Her phrasing and tone make my hackles rise, and I glare at her briefly. "This is Meghan's best friend. She's staying with me for a while as she settles into her new job and finds an apartment."

"Oh, I remember you telling me that." She doesn't wait for a formal introduction, turning away from Keaton to look at me. "What do you recommend?"

"You've been here before. I'm certain you must have a few favorites." I sound abrupt, and I can't hide my irritation with her. In an exaggerated fashion, I say, "Keaton, this is Vanessa, my business partner. Vanessa, this is Keaton."

Keaton holds out her hand, and Vanessa ignores it for a moment. She finally blinks and looks up as Keaton starts to drop her hand, clearly trying to seem as though she didn't see Keaton's hand until then. I'm not sure why she's acting this way, but it displeases me.

Vanessa and I normally work well together. She has a sharp, aggressive manner often required in our line of work to acquire new clients. I wouldn't call her a friend necessarily, but her brisk attitude doesn't normally irritate me. It's not usually as blatant though. I get the sense she's taken an immediate dislike to Keaton for no good reason.

"Keaton is an unusual name for a woman. Or anyone," says Vanessa with a laugh that has a jagged edge to it.

I wince on Keaton's behalf, but she doesn't seem to think much of it. She shrugs her shoulders. "My mother was a poetry professor. John Keats and Emily Dickinson were her favorites, so she combined them into my name."

"It must be a nice talking point to make people think you're interesting."

Keaton frowns at Vanessa's words, and I scowl at her. She's carefully avoiding my eyes, and I'm confused by it.

I notice Keaton has finished, and I decide if Vanessa wants to be rude, two can play that game. "Are you finished, Keaton?" At her nod, I say, "Why don't we get out of here? You must be tired after your first day."

Keaton slants an uncertain look at Vanessa, but then she nods. "I wouldn't mind an early night."

"You're leaving?" Vanessa sounds irate as she glares at me. "I just got here."

"That's true, but you couldn't have anticipated eating with us. We wouldn't want to hold you up, since you're likely meeting someone. You might as well take our table though." I deliver it all smoothly, as though I'm only thinking of her, but by the way Vanessa's eyes narrow, I'm certain she's gotten the message that I'm annoyed with her behavior, and I'm not going to subject Keaton to it any longer.

I settle the bill for myself and Keaton, and we're strolling away from the restaurant a short time later. She's noticeably subdued, and I take her hand without thought, squeezing lightly. She gasps softly, and I hastily let go of her hand. "I'm sorry about Vanessa. Sometimes, she gets in a mood or something."

She arches a brow, but she just nods. "Thank you for a lovely dinner."

"I'm sorry you didn't get to try the tiramisu."

She shrugs her shoulders. "That's all right. I remember seeing a gelato stand on the way here."

I groan at the thought even as she increases her pace. I start walking faster to match, and we soon reach the gelato stand. She orders a huge dish of it, and the clerk looks at me. "Whatcha having, buddy?"

"Nothing for me." Keaton frowns, and her frown deepens when I hand over cash as she reaches for her purse.

"I can buy my own gelato," she says a few minutes later on the way back to the apartment.

I shrug a shoulder. "Yeah, I'm sure you can, but you had your hands full between the purse and the gelato."

She hesitates for a moment and then nods. "Thanks again."

I shrug off the expression of gratitude as we enter the building and take the elevator back to my floor. It feels second nature to rest my hand against her lower back as we walk together, and we reach the door all too soon. I don't mind being home, but I'm sad to lose the reason I had been lightly touching her back. It's ridiculous to get so much pleasure from such light interaction.

When we enter the apartment, she takes her bag of gelato straight to the coffee table and sits down, patting the cushion beside her. For reasons I can't explain, I'm strangely reluctant to take that spot, while simultaneously eager to do so. It feels like a mistake I want to make in the worst way as I cross the room and sit beside her.

Chapter Four

I TRY TO PRETEND I'M not aware of his proximity as I open the bag and unpack the large bowl of gelato, discovering the cart owner slipped in two spoons. I hold one out to Evan, content to share the treat. Even as he takes it, he shakes his head. "I really shouldn't. My metabolism's not as fast as it used to be."

I stare him in astonishment for a moment, surprised to hear he has any insecurities or concerns about his body. "You look perfect to me." I blurt without a filter, but I can feel my cheeks flushing with embarrassment at the admission. I clear my throat and try again. "I mean, you're clearly going to the gym and taking care of yourself. You have muscles on muscles. I doubt a little gelato is going to hurt you."

He looks confused for a moment, as though he doesn't know what to say, but then he chuckles. "I suppose you've convinced me." He takes the spoon to dig into his side of the container.

The gelato is as creamy as I anticipated, and I enjoy it, but my face feels hotter as I unexpectedly imagine how it would be to drizzle melting gelato across his chest and flat stomach before licking it away. I haven't seen him without a shirt in some time, but I'm certain he's as toned as he seems under his clothes, and it's easy enough to imagine how it would feel to slide my tongue along the curves and ridges of his abdomen.

It causes me to inhale sharply, and in the process, I choke on a bite of gelato. It feels like it's stuck in my throat as I gasp, leaning forward. He rubs my back in a soothing motion, which feels nice, but it does nothing to help me start breathing properly again. Everything about

Evan has a way of stealing my breath and turning me into a sodden mess of sensations.

Somehow, I finally get down the lump of gelato, and I can fully breathe again. I cough a few times, and he seems nothing but concerned. For my part, I'm embarrassed by my inability to eat. He must think I'm a complete moron, and I just keep giving him reasons to reach that conclusion. With a shake of my head, disgusted with myself, I clear my throat one last time and stand up. "I think I'm done with the gelato. Do you want more?"

He shakes his head, so I take the bowl into the kitchen and dispose of the rest. There's not enough to be worth saving. After that, I drink a glass of water, aware of him leaning in the doorway watching me. I'm certain it's enough to cause me to choke again, but I somehow manage to swallow like a normal human being before putting the glass in the dishwasher. "Thank you for being there and listening tonight, Evan. I think I'm going to go to bed now." I'm eager to escape before I make an even bigger fool of myself.

He nods and steps back as I pass through the doorway between the kitchen and the hall. I could probably squeeze by without touching him, but I can't resist the temptation, so I let my body lightly brush against his for a moment before stepping into the hallway. I turn away from him and walk to my room, going straight for the bathroom. There's a soaker tub that's calling my name, so I turn the water as hot as I can stand it, sprinkle in some bath oil, and soon submerge myself.

At first, I don't allow any thoughts to cross my brain or coalesce into something more solid. It's relaxed notions that ping off my subconscious without registering until an image starts to solidify in my mind.

I see Evan kneeling on the floor on his knees. For a moment, I'm uncomfortable with the idea, because he's not a man meant for kneeling and submission. I soon realize my brain is picturing him that way for a reason, and it has nothing to do a submission, except maybe my own.

I can imagine his face between my legs, his tongue tracing the length of my slit before his lips tighten gently around my clit. It's all in my head, but it feels realistic enough to cause a jolt to go through me, then my hand drops from my stomach to move lower.

My folds are slick even in the bathwater, and I slide my finger inside. I'm picturing it as his tongue, and my fantasy Evan knows exactly the best spots to explore first. I close my eyes and gasp lightly while touching myself. It feels so real, and the mental images are so vivid.

I know it's crazy, and I shouldn't be thinking this way about him, but I let the fantasy play out in my head as my fingers do the work. I'm imagining his performance until I come with a small cry a short time later.

Once I'm satisfied, I feel embarrassed for the thoughts, and guilt starts to eat at me. Evan would probably be appalled if he realized I once had a crush on him, and it hasn't dissipated nearly as well as I'd expected. It's threatening to roar back to life, and I'm afraid it won't be something as benign as a crush this time. We're living in close quarters, and though I know I'm not his type, and he probably considers me way too young, I could probably be dumb enough to fall in love with him if I let myself do it.

Ruthlessly, I force myself to imagine his pretty business partner, with her razor-cut black hair, cool gray eyes, and contemptuous expression. She seems far more put together and polished than I can ever hope to be, and I'm certain she's just Evan's type.

I don't know that they're involved with each other, and Evan seemed annoyed with her, but I can't discount the possibility. Even if he's not with Vanessa, who clearly wants to be with him, that's the kind of woman he's going to go for. I'm totally fine with who I am, but I'm never going to be a fashion plate or supermodel, and that dose of reality is just what I need as I get out of the tub, shower quickly, and go to my room.

I slide under the covers without bothering to dress, closing my eyes and focusing on going to sleep, though it's not even nine o'clock yet. As stressful as the day was, I can feel sleep starting to creep over me, and I tell myself I have a handle on the situation. I can ignore the attraction I feel, and I can certainly keep from letting it spill over or influencing my choices. I feel confident and composed by the time I fall asleep, certain I'm not going to let myself fall for my best friend's brother.

I dream about him.

Chapter Five

Evan

I SPENT THE LAST FEW days voluntarily avoiding Keaton as much as possible, but my luck runs out tonight when I come home from the office and find her curled up in a miserable ball on the couch. Her cheeks are flushed, and her eyes are red. She's holding a crumpled tissue in her hand, and it takes a heartless bastard to be able to walk away from that. Some of my business rivals might class me that way, but I can't be so ruthless with her, even though I'm avoiding her for her sake.

Or so I told myself. She doesn't need the awkwardness of realizing I'm attracted to her and drooling after her. It will just make her uncomfortable to stay with me, and I'm trying to do the right thing by steering clear.

In spite of that, I walk over to the couch and take the cushion beside her. "What's wrong?"

"Mr. Smith fired me today." She sniffles before blowing her nose with a honking sound.

I scowl on her behalf. "That's ridiculous. He's barely given you any time to prove yourself."

She shrugs a shoulder. "He keeps finding fault with everything I do, but I'm sure part of it is because I declined his casual invitation to lunch yesterday. I did it as politely as possible, and I had hoped it would be enough to satisfy him that I'm not going to get involved, but this feels like retaliation. Either that, or he's really determined that his nephew will have the job." She sniffs again, but when she blows her nose this time, it's a more sedate sound.

"We'll get an attorney."

She waves a hand dismissively. "There's no point in going that route. I'll take years to settle, and maybe I'll win, but it will probably put a black mark on my record."

"Sexual harassment is illegal." I frown at her as I say it.

She snorts. It's not at all dignified, but there's something adorable about it. "Being illegal and being enforceable are two different things, which I'm sure you know. I don't have the time, energy, or money to fight it. Besides, I really didn't like the job anyway." She blinks at that admission. "Maybe it's for the best."

"Now you can find something you like better."

Keaton shakes her head. "I won't, not in this economy. It took months to find this job, and I wasn't even set on New York. I applied in lots of different places, and this was the only offer I got. I'm going to have to go home, and I might have to return to my job as a barista." She grimaces.

I grimace for her, imagining how she must be feeling. "There are other jobs."

"Not for someone with a basic bachelor's degree and not enough experience. There are about a million of us out there, so I'm not under any illusion I'll be able to get hired. I'll probably go back to my old job and work on my videogame on the side as I have been doing. It was working, mostly." She frowns. "Except student loans. Repayment..." She groans.

I lucked out and got a full scholarship, but it wasn't luck so much as hard work. I imagine my parents would've helped her pay for college too, as they would've offered to do for me if I hadn't had most of my expenses covered, but I imagine Keaton said no. "Are you planning to open your own design company then?"

She shrugs a shoulder. "Why not? I might not get anywhere, but it seems like the best option." She frowns. "Do you know how long it took me to be able to drink coffee again after I stopped working at the coffee shop? I'm going to miss that, but once I'm surrounded by it all day, I just can't drink it."

I shake my head. "You're going to stay right here and work on your game."

Her eyes narrow as she tips her head. "It's an interesting idea, but even though the salary must be better here in New York for a barista, it can't possibly be enough to support myself."

"You don't have to worry about that. You can stay in the apartment rent-free while you're building your game."

She frowns. "I can't accept that."

Realizing she's not going to go for what I'm suggesting, I change tactics slightly. "I think you're misunderstanding me. It's not a charity thing. It's an investment in your future company. We can draw up papers to make it official, but I'd expect at least a ten percent share." It's a number I pick randomly, hoping I sound businesslike enough to convince her it's my sole thought.

She frowns, still looking uncertain. "You don't even like video games. Why would you want to invest in my company?"

"It's not about if I like them, but if other people do. It's a booming market, and I've been looking to diversify my investments. It seems like a good opportunity, and this is a low-stakes investment for me from the start."

Keaton shakes her head. "If it fails, you'll get ten percent of nothing."

"It's a risk I'm willing to take. There aren't that many investment opportunities that come along without requiring a significant amount upfront. I'd be a fool not to go after this idea." My conscience twinges for a moment, because I know full well it's not a business opportunity I'm after. The more time I spend with Keaton, the more time I want to spend with her.

"I guess we could do this. I don't know though. It feels like I'm taking advantage of you, Evan."

I reach out, putting a hand over hers. "You aren't. We're practically family."

She nods, falling silent for a minute. When she looks down, she's nibbling on her lower lip, and her hand is tense under mine.

She takes a deep breath and looks up at me again, as though she's reached a decision. "You don't feel like family."

I flinch at that. "I know I haven't spent as much time with you as the rest of my family, but you're Meghan's best friend. I want to help you."

"Just because I'm Meghan's best friend?" She tilts her head slightly as she asks me that, as though considering something weighty.

I start to confirm it, but it isn't entirely the truth. I had no problem helping Meghan's friend by letting her stay in my place for a few weeks until she got her own apartment, but I know I'm going beyond the bounds of any kind of familial obligation with my offer. Obviously, Keaton knows it too. My voice is husky when I say, "No."

"You don't consider me like a sister?" Her lips are parted, and she seems to be holding her breath as she awaits my answer.

I shake my head. "Of course not."

Rather than look hurt or upset, she appears relieved. "I don't see you as a brother either, Evan."

There's silence between us for a moment, and then she moves quickly, as though she's gathering her nerves and forcing herself to act. She stretches forward, arching her neck to lift her face, and her lips press against mine.

It's a shy, almost tentative kiss, and I hold out responding for a moment. The way her lips coaxingly move against mine, so soft and pliant, makes it impossible to resist, and I lower my head a bit more, bringing my mouth more firmly against hers. I take control of the kiss, and it escalates to something far different and more intense than the shy kiss she offered.

As my tongue breaches the seam of her lips, and the taste of her fills my mouth, I realize exactly what I'm doing. Maybe I could continue on. Maybe she isn't disgusted by the idea of me being attracted to her, but she's still Meghan's best friend, and she's been entrusted to my care while she's here.

Though every instinct I have protests pulling away, I make myself do it and get to my feet. I can't look at her for the moment, or I might surrender to the temptation to pull her into my arms again. Instead, I turn away from her and stride from the room, stopping in the foyer to grasp a tabletop to steady myself.

My knuckles are white from the strength of my hold, and there's a sharp pain, but it does little to permeate my clouded senses. All I can think about is Keaton with her lips parted and how she tastes. It takes everything I have not to turn around and walk back into the room.

Chapter Six

I ALMOST PRAY I CAN die from embarrassment for a moment as I sit there after he stands up and walks away. He didn't even look at me, and he seemed to be having a difficult time keeping himself in check. No doubt, he's currently disgusted by my actions and trying to think of a gentle way to tell me he's not interested.

I snort as I get to my feet. Too little too late for gentle. The way he pulled himself away from me and stepped out of the room speaks volumes, and I have no interest in his "let me down easy" speech that he's surely currently composing.

With that thought in mind, I hurry to the room I've been using and take my suitcase from the closet. I have it half-filled before I hear a rustling in the doorway. I look up briefly to see him standing there, but I quickly look away. I find it impossible to maintain eye contact at the moment.

He seems awkward when he shifts from one foot to the other as his broad shoulders partially fill the doorway. "May I talk to you, Keaton?"

I shrug a shoulder and nod jerkily. "Might as well. I'll be here for a few more minutes." I sound almost passive-aggressive, and I wince at that.

"I'm sorry about that. I shouldn't have kissed you."

That's enough to make me pause in the process of dumping a handful of bras into the suitcase. I stare at him in shock for a moment, my mouth gaping like a moron. "I don't think you're the one you kissed anyone. That was me. I'm sorry."

He waves a hand. "Why don't we just chalk it up to one of those moments of madness?" He looks disapproving as he gazes at my suitcase. "There's certainly no reason for you to walk out."

He makes it sound like I'm abandoning him. "I'm just going home. I think that's best. I have a good plan."

"There's no justification for you to go home. You can still stay here. The kiss was foolish, but it's not going to be repeated."

You can say that again. As humiliating as that experience was, there's no way I'll try to repeat it. "Really, I'd rather go back to the Middletons. As much as I hate living off their charity for a short time, I can make it work. Maybe I can find a job near Meghan's campus, and she'll be living there for her master's degree. We can be roommates or something."

He's frowning. "I already offered to invest in your business."

I wave a hand. "What business? It's just a pipe dream really. I have to have practical and immediate options."

"You can immediately continue with your game if you stay here. No strings attached... Other than you'll give me ten percent of your future company."

I frown. "And that makes me nothing more than charity for you too. I appreciate the offer, but I'm leaving."

He stares at me for a moment, looking like he still wants to argue. He's poised with his lips open, but after a moment, his shoulder sinks slightly, and he sighs heavily instead. "I can't force you to stay, but I think you're making a mistake and losing an amazing opportunity."

I shrug a shoulder. "It won't be my first mistake or my last."

Evan still seems like he wants to argue with me, but after a moment, he shakes his head and steps back. "I'll leave you to pack then." He sounds melancholy about it, like he's sorry to lose me.

I tell myself I'm just projecting that, because he certainly never had me. When I offered myself practically on a platter with an apple in my mouth, he turned me down.

A treacherous voice in the back of my mind whispers the reminder that he kissed me before he stepped away, but I tell myself that doesn't matter. Ultimately, that he got up and left the room to avoid me tells me everything I need to know.

After he leaves, I get the rest of my items packed, glad I didn't bring much with me. I'd planned to rent a furnished apartment, so I only brought enough clothes for a couple weeks and a few other sundries. I'm packed and ready to leave within an hour. I reach for my phone to secure a ticket with the emergency funds I have saved on a credit card for just that purpose as the doorbell rings. I don't bother to investigate, certain it's not for me.

Chapter Seven

Evan

I'M TRYING TO THINK of a way to convince Keaton to change her mind as I pace my living room, pausing periodically to stare out at the view below. The city is lit up, and it normally makes me cheerful, but tonight, nothing can have that effect. I'm too disappointed that she's planning to leave already.

I have only myself to blame, and I know that. If I hadn't pulled away from her kiss, this evening could've played out very differently. I might even now be holding her in my arms. I was shocked to realize she has similar emotions for me, and she's definitely attracted to me. I should be too old for her and too far away from her life experiences and interests, so it's gratifying to know she shares the attraction. So why the hell did I pull away? What was I thinking?

I shake my head in disgust. I don't know what I was thinking when I left her. I should've deepened the kiss instead of allowing guilt to get the best of me. I have no reason to feel guilty. She's an adult, and she kissed me of her own volition. I should've just ignored the twinge of conscience that had me imagining what my parents would say if they found out I had taken advantage of Keaton.

They'd be sorely disappointed in me, and they'd be rightfully angry on her behalf. Though I don't get home as much as I'd like to these days, I'm still close to my parents, and their good opinion matters to me. And it matters to Keaton as well, so it seemed like the sensible thing to do.

I might've had good intentions with pulling away, but now I curse myself for having done so. All my intentions did were ensure she's packing right now to leave me. Maybe it's not as intimate as that, but it certainly feels personal. I want to fall down on my knees and beg her to stay, which is certainly not my style. I'm still trying to think of a way to convince her to change her mind when the doorbell rings.

For a moment, I'm afraid it's a taxi service or the like, someone she's called to take her to the airport, to take her away from me. Surely, she isn't leaving already? I'm not ready to have her out of my life just yet. I need more time to prepare. With that in mind, I stride to the door and pull it open, prepared to send whoever is on the other side away.

Instead of a driver or a stranger, Vanessa stands there. I'm reasonably certain Keaton didn't call her for a ride, so when she starts to ease past, I step aside. "I didn't expect to see you here tonight." As I speak, she undoes her coat and hands it to me. I hang it on the coatrack, uncomfortably aware of just how close she is in the confines of the small space.

I can't exactly knock her aside with my elbow, so I have to wait for her to move. She seems to be making it her life's work, but she finally eases away and takes a seat on one of the wingbacks. She crosses her legs at the knee, swinging her foot casually. It's a shapely leg, and any man would recognize the beauty of it, but I'm in no mood to appreciate Vanessa's natural beauty or her presence in my apartment this evening. "What do you need?" I cross my arms over my chest as I ask.

"I came for the Ferguson file."

I frown at her. "I could've just emailed that to you."

She tips her head slightly. "I much prefer to look at the brochures myself and feel the texture. We don't want to send out something cheap."

I shrug a shoulder, wanting to ask why this task couldn't wait until tomorrow. Vanessa's like me, often driven to work long hours, but there's nothing in the Ferguson campaign that requires an urgent examination of the paper quality this time of night.

"Where's your little guest?"

My teeth set on edge at the condescending tone she uses. "Keaton is in her room."

"You mean your guestroom. It's not really her room."

I turn to face her, forgetting about the Ferguson file as I prop a hip against the wall, still having my arms crossed over my chest. "What exactly is your problem with Keaton, Vanessa?"

Her eyes widen, and she seems like she's going to play dumb for a moment. It's a surprise when she blinks, her expression becoming cooler. "I have nothing against the child per se, but it's bad for your image to have a young girl living here. Our clients and business associates won't know she's like a sister to you." She shakes her head while clicking her tongue. "All they're going to see is a sad old man with a young girl. They're going to assume you're her sugar daddy."

I blink at her, too stunned to speak for a moment. "First of all, it's only a twelve-year age difference. I'm hardly old enough to be her sugar daddy, Vanessa. I doubt anybody's going to jump to that conclusion."

She shrugs her shoulders. "We're successful, and our company is doing well, but you know how much networking and our image influences client selection and the confidence they have in us. No one wants to be in business with a pedophile."

I'm starting to get genuinely angry now. "For fuck's sake, Vanessa, Keaton is an adult woman. You're being ridiculous."

"I'm not the one concerned. I just think our clients might not look at it the same way I do. I know she's your sister in all ways but biological, but they don't know that."

I stare at her for a moment, just until she starts to shift uneasily. I let the silence lengthen for another long second as I eye her, appraising why she's here, and the truth behind her words. She's spinning me a tale, and I can recognize that. I've seen her in action enough to know she's giving me her sales routine, though I'm not entirely sure what she's trying to sell me. Whatever it is, I'm not buying it. "I think you should go now, Vanessa. I'll get that file to you in the morning when I'm done with it."

She looks startled for a moment as she gets to her feet. Her expression reveals she's offended. "I don't see why you're so angry with me. I'm just speaking the truth."

"You're speaking your version of the truth." As I say that, I walked toward her, putting my hand slightly less than gently on her forearm to urge her to the front door while grabbing her coat with my other hand. It's only as she starts to step through that she turns back to look at me, lips parted as though about to speak. I don't want to hear it. "For the record, Keaton isn't my sister, and I don't view her as one."

With those words, I gently close the door in her face and engage the lock. I chuckle a little bit as I walk away, imagining how she's going to spend her night. She'll be thinking I'm with Keaton, and that obviously bothers her. I had no idea she might've been developing any feelings for me besides professional. We're hardly even friends. We certainly don't spend time together outside of the office except for business reasons, though we have made some work trips together. We do spend a lot of time together at the office, and I can't believe I never picked up on the fact she's attracted to me.

Or maybe she's not even overly attracted to me. Maybe she's just feeling possessive because she thinks I'll lose focus on the business if I get distracted with Keaton. It could be a possibility but seems like a remote one, and it doesn't ring true for her motivations anyway. This feels more personal on her part, and it's embarrassing to realize she might be attached to me in a way I'm not attached to her.

I stop walking as I cringe, realizing Keaton is probably feeling this very thing right now. When I got up and walked out of the room without speaking to her about the kiss, she probably interpreted it as a lack of interest on my part rather than my attempt to regain control. I groan as I plant a palm against the wall in the hallway, bracing myself. No wonder she's leaving. She feels a mix of embarrassment and rejection, so it's a wonder she was able to talk to me at all.

I hasten down the hallway, anxious to convince her it's definitely not a one-sided attraction. It's probably not the best idea I've ever had to confirm that. I don't know what will happen if things progress along a natural course, but I can't let her to continue to believe I don't want her.

I knock on her door, getting an unenthusiastic, "It's unlocked." I turn the knob and step inside, dismayed to see her suitcase is already packed. She's sitting at the desk her phone in hand, and I'm sure she's browsing the airlines. A glance at the window behind her, which reflects her screen, confirms my supposition. "Don't book a flight." I speak firmly.

Her finger stalls on the laptop for a moment as she looks up at me. "We've already had this discussion. I'll be better off in Michigan."

"I don't want you to leave." I cross the room to stand beside her desk, looking down at her. "That's the last thing I want." As I speak, I stroke the back of my fingers down her cheek before moving my hand to tangle in her hair. I gently stroke the brown locks as her eyes close, and she leans into the touch. She reminds me of an affectionate little cat, and I smile.

After a moment, she freezes and jerks away. "I have to. You wouldn't understand, but it's the best thing for me."

I don't like the resolve in her tone, as though she's made up her mind and won't change it. I know how stubborn she can be sometimes, and I realize my only hope of getting through the block she's putting between us is to be completely honest.

I kneel beside her, and she looks at me with some apprehension. "I stopped kissing you because I was trying to do the right thing, not because I didn't want to kiss you."

Her eyes widen, and she seems to be having difficulty comprehending my words for a moment. "I... What?"

I smirk, unable to deny a certain sense of smugness at being able to reduce her to a practically nonverbal state. "I want you, Keaton. I was thinking about all the reasons why that could go wrong, or how my parents and Meghan would feel, and that's why I stepped away."

"Oh." She licks her lips as she looks down. "Those fears are still valid."

"Maybe." I move my hand from her hair to her chin, gently urging her to look up at me. "I don't want to regret letting you go though. We can't make our decisions based on how others will feel when it matters so much to both of us. If you don't want me, you absolutely should say so right now. I won't hold it against you, and I won't be angry. Even after that kiss, if you decide it was just a foolish mistake and tell me that, I'll accept your word on the matter. I'm not interested in forcing you into anything you don't want, but I'm imploring you to make the determination for yourself and not because others might not understand or like it."

She blinks, and her tongue darts out to moisten her lips again. It's all I can do to keep from leaning forward and snagging it between my teeth before lightly nipping her. I groan at the thought, and the sound is full of desire.

Her eyes widen and darken in a similar way, and I can tell she's feeling the longing between us. Still, I have to let her make the first move, so I hold absolutely still, fingers tipped under her chin while my other hand is clenched into a fist at my side just from the struggle to maintain control.

"I really don't want to leave."

"Then stay. No strings attached." I look deep into her eyes, praying she'll find me sincere. "I really do want you to stay, and the room is still yours if you want it, and we can handle this however you want. We can stay friends if that's what you want, or we can explore being more."

She looks faintly apprehensive as she leans forward, but her voice emerges sounding clear and confident. "I've never wanted to be just your friend, Evan. The feelings I've had for you have deepened and changed, but they were never just sisterly or even friendly."

It causes a funny stirring sensation in my stomach to hear her confirm that. I clear my throat, wishing I could tell her it's the same for me. "I'm sorry to say that I didn't really notice you until now. You were just my sister's friend...much younger than me friend," I add. "I think it probably would've been weird if I'd noticed you in such a way."

She laughs. "Very weird, so I'm relieved you didn't. I never expected you to see me as anything more than Meghan's friend though."

"You've grown into an amazing woman, Keaton, and I'd be blind not to notice." I lean forward, still intent on letting her make the first move, but actively encouraging her to do so.

After another hesitation, she leans forward as well, and her lips brush against mine. The kiss starts out gently, just like last time, and I let her set the pace. It's almost a surprise when her touches move from curious and savoring to wild and needy. As her passion ramps up, so does mine, and I stand up as I urge her to her feet.

We don't break the kiss as we move backward toward the bed. I had every intention of taking this slowly, giving her space and letting her set whatever pace felt comfortable, but it's difficult to make that offer when she's tearing at the buttons of my shirt with clear, animalistic need. I know I should probably offer to ease back and slow down, but Keaton doesn't seem any more interested in that idea than I am.

Chapter Eight

Keaton

I'VE NEVER FELT THIS way before. I've had a couple of lovers, including Chase, who I dated for a year, but they never left me feeling like I was dancing on the edge of a precipice and eager to jump off the edge.

With a whimper, I tug his shirt free from his pants after wrestling the buttons into submission. It doesn't take much to remove the fabric after that, and as he settles atop me, his bare torso feels good. It'll be even better when I'm naked too.

He must share the thought, because he tugs at the hem of my shirt. I lean up to assist him, and the plain cotton is soon over my head and on the floor. My bra joins it, and he returns to my arms, lying atop me while supporting his weight.

We're kissing again, our lips and tongues clashing and stroking, as though we're making love and conquering each other simultaneously. If I dwell on it, I'll feel daunted by how much experience he must surely have compared to me, so I don't think. I just concentrate on feeling.

I rake my nails down his sides before digging them gently into his back. His breath hisses between his parted lips, washing over my chin as he jerks and presses his back against me. He must like a little pain with his pleasure. I strain upward and nip his chin.

He growls low in his throat as one of his hands clenches in my hair, tugging back my head to expose my throat. Maybe I should be afraid of the feral passion he's displaying, but I'm too turned on for fear. When he nips me in retaliation on the column of my throat before his teeth nibble a path to the bend of my shoulder, I squeal and arch my hips. He spends an inordinate amount of time exploring my neck with his teeth, lips, and tongue before he homes in on my earlobe.

I've never had a man explore that area, but I soon learn why it's considered an erogenous zone. Each little nip of his teeth sends a corresponding pulse through my pussy, and I shake and squeeze my thighs to alleviate the ache. It does nothing. "Evan, please..."

He seems reluctant as he pulls away to look down at me. "Tell me what you want, Keaton."

"You."

His lips curve into a small smirk. "I know, but how."

"I want you inside me." I blush as I look up at him. I'm certain he wants more than that, but I'm not used to much talking at all during sex, let alone sexy talk.

He grins, but he seems ready to give me what I want, at least until I realize he's repositioning me not for his cock to enter me, but for his mouth to settle over my mound. I grasp his hair to anchor myself as his tongue sweeps through my folds. He's not exploring so much as claiming his territory. I feel marked by him as he sucks forcefully on my clit. It should hurt, but it just feels good instead. I whimper and arch my hips.

His mouth is voracious on me, but he still manages to be gentle while he's devouring me. It's a form of controlled violence, almost, as he ravishes me but never hurts me. He seems to know instinctively what I'll crave, and where to touch me. It's uncannily like the fantasy I had of him in the bathtub.

Stars dance behind my eyes as the universe fractalizes around me. Pleasure courses through me, making it impossible to breathe for a moment. I clutch him against me as he tries to move away, and he firmly sets me aside. I whimper at the loss of contact and reach for him, but he's soon back to soothe me.

"Hush, Keaton. I've got you." He kisses me as he nudges apart my thighs with his knee.

I cling to him, needing that more than I can explain or express. I need to have his arms around me, to feel him holding me tightly like this.

He's moving a hand between my thighs, and it takes me a minute to realize he's putting on a condom. In a hazy, distant way, I'm impressed he's managing the task with one hand, but I'm too incoherent with desire to offer to assist or even move away to give him more room.

Finally, his cock presses against my opening. I'm wet and waiting for him, but he doesn't enter yet. I glare up at him. "What're you waiting for? An invitation?"

He laughs. The bastard has the nerve to be amused by my frustration and need. I want to tell him off, but I can't think straight for the necessity to have him inside me. The orgasm he gave me was just enough to whet my appetite, but I want the full show now.

"I want to make sure you're frantic, aching, and dripping for me." His husky tone makes my pussy pulse. "Are you, Keaton? Are you aching for me to be inside you?"

I nod frantically, no longer constrained by embarrassment or reluctance. "Please fuck me, Evan."

He chuckles and starts to sink inside me. "Thank god, because I can't hold out another minute."

I'm pleased to realize he's as affected as I am as my body accepts his length. I twitch and adjust to his unexpected girth, unsure I can take it for a second. A partial rotation of my hips and an angle adjustment from him steals away the doubt as my insides curve around him. He feels perfect inside me then, and I realize just how inadequate my previous lovers have been.

He starts to rock slowly in and out of me, but I have no patience for that. I clamp my legs around his hips and dig my heels into his buttocks. I strain and press against him, urging him to surrender his careful control. He fights for a moment, with sweat beading on his forehead. Finally, with a low grunt of surrender, he surges inside me and starts pounding my body with all the pent-up ferocity I crave.

We're frantic and needful, but we fit together just right. It could be forever or a few minutes before my channel convulses around him, and his cock stiffens inside me. I feel the warmth of his release through the condom, which coaxes another orgasm from me. I cry out his name with a strangled sound as I cling to him while riding the waves of my second release. It shouldn't be, but it's somehow more intense than the first.

I'm barely sentient when it's over. I collapse against the bed, clinging to him even when he shifts to make sure we're more comfortable. I can't let go of him, and I hold onto him as though he's the only anchor in my world. Staring into his eyes, I find it easy to believe he is in that moment.

Chapter Nine

Evan

AFTER WE'RE BOTH SATED, I hold her in my arms, knowing I should regret this, but I don't. She shifts slightly, and I think Keaton is trying to pull away, so my arms tighten reflexively around her. Instead, she's just getting more comfortable, and I'm still surprised by my reaction. I'm not usually the cuddling type, and though I'll endure it for a lover who favors it, I usually prefer to distance myself as quickly as possible. I don't feel that need with Keaton.

"Did we just make a huge mistake?" She looks up at me from where her cheek is pressed against my chest.

I hesitate for a moment, formulating a response. "It doesn't feel like it."

She sighs, but she also nods. "I don't feel like it was a mistake either, but I'm still sort of surprised it happened. I've had a crush on you for years, but I guess I never really considered the reality that it might move beyond that someday. You always seemed perfectly unattainable."

I frown at that, along with the revelation that she's had a crush on me. I had no indication of that or any hint of her attraction until she moved in. I'm not sure whether to be flattered or embarrassed, since I never noticed. I can feel a mixture of both, I decide. Rather than focusing on that, I say, "I felt this tug toward you from the moment I saw you standing on my doorstep. I guess I'm not surprised this happened. It feels inevitable." I enjoy the way her eyes widen as I make the admission.

Her lips curve upward for a moment, and then her expression darkens. "Meghan won't like this."

I sigh. "Neither will my folks." As I speak, I trail my fingers through her brown locks, liking the way they look spread across my stomach.

Her voice is hoarse for a moment when she says, "I don't want to do anything to hurt Lily, Everett, or Meghan."

"Neither do I." Still, my hand tightens around her hair. "I'm not willing to make myself unhappy either."

She looks up at me again, biting her lip. "Are you saying that forgetting this ever happened and never doing it again will make you unhappy?"

I haven't had a chance to really analyze my feelings, or what I think of the situation, but I instinctively answer, "Yes." It's the truth. The idea of forgetting this happened, or of never having Keaton again, sends a pang through my chest.

"It's the same for me." She flushes at the admission, as though uncomfortable discussing her feelings. I can relate, since I usually avoid that kind of discussion like the plague. "But your family..."

"I don't suppose we have to rush right off and tell them what we've done." I make this suggestion tentatively, not liking the idea of hiding our changed relationship. Dishonesty doesn't sit well with me, but I see the value in not rushing out to share either. I can well imagine my parents' reaction if I call them up and tell them I just slept with Keaton. Meghan would probably react equally badly, so I doubt Keaton's eager to tell them either.

She still looks uncertain as she nods. "I guess we don't have to. I mean, this might not even be more than a short-term thing."

I should feel relieved that she's put that out there, revealing she doesn't expect anything permanent from me, and she's not looking for a commitment. Instead, I feel angry and possessive at the idea of her ending this thing between us. It's probably insane, but I'm on the verge of telling her I won't be the one to walk away. Somehow, I manage to still the impulse and redirect those feelings by pulling her into my arms and taking her again.

I STAND OUTSIDE THE building where Keaton used to work the next day. It took five minutes on Google to discover what Bill Smith looks like, and now I wait for him. My assistant was annoyed when I called to tell her to push back my meetings, but I don't care. Haley can deal with that, and I have something more important to handle.

He finally emerges, and I see a young woman standing beside him. She's walking with him, but her posture suggests she's reluctant to be there. I have no qualms about moving forward to interrupt them. I face Smith after nodding to the young lady. "I need to speak with you." I speak in a stern fashion, not giving him a choice.

The young woman looks relieved as she scurries away, which makes Bill Smith frown in annoyance before he looks at me. "Who are you?"

"My name is Evan Middleton, but that's not what you need to know."

Smith's portly face contorts into an expression of confusion. "What do I need to know then?" He sounds slightly indulgent.

"I'm the one who's going to destroy you."

His expression changes, and his tone loses any hint of pandering. "What are you talking about?"

"Maybe you should consider yourself lucky that Keaton doesn't want to deal with the hassle of telling HR what you've done or a drawn-out lawsuit, but I don't intend to leave you feeling grateful for anything."

His eyes narrow, and he looks nervous, but he's still going for bluster. "I have no idea what you're talking about. Who is this Keaton?" He gives a big production of frowning. "We recently had a programmer by that name, come to think of it. She was incompetent."

"She turned down your advances, so you fired her." I cross my arms over my chest as I glare at him, daring him to deny it.

"I would never—"

I put up a hand. "Yeah, you would. I absolutely believe her, especially after doing a little digging of my own." That was a slight exaggeration, since I actually had one of the security consultants our firm retains look into him, but it's easy to see there's been a pattern of young women moving through his department in rapid turnover over the last few years.

"I don't know who you are, or what you think you're doing, but—"

"I'm ending your ability to keep hurting young ladies. I just happen to know Dane Beaumont." And by happen to know, I live in his building, and my company has handled a campaign for one of his companies in the past.

His eyes widen, and he looks suddenly nauseated. "What does my boss have to do with anything?"

"Technically, he's more like your boss's boss's boss's boss, isn't he?" I ask in a neutral fashion but give him a lethal grin. "He's a good friend of mine, and when I informed him just what you've been up to, he was happy to handle the matter."

Smith starts to sweat, and I grin as I see Dane approaching, as arranged. I smile at him and hold out a hand to shake as he reaches us. "Impeccable timing, Dane."

"Not entirely. If I had good timing, this piece of crap would have been fired long ago."

Smith stiffens at the words, and he looks at Dane with open misery. "I don't know what they're talking about. I've never—"

"Save it." Dane speaks harshly, and he's frowning heavily. "You're out. Security is packing up your desk right now, and don't even think about asking for a severance package. What you're due will be divided among the six women we've been able to identify as victimized enough by you to either be fired or quit over the last few years you've been in charge of the department."

The man pales and sways. "What? It's not like they sued. Why do you even care?"

"Because you're a piece of excrement, and you taint my company. Walk away now while you still can." Dane cracks his knuckles in a menacing fashion, and with his size and muscles, there's little doubt he can follow through on the unspoken threat.

I have places to be, so I leave Dane to handle the last of the theatrics, looking forward to sharing the news with Keaton.

I do just that later, once I reach home for the day. I find she's already ordered us takeout. I sit down on the couch beside her and say, "I have good news."

She arches a brow as she hands me a pair of chopsticks and a carton. "What's that?"

"Bill Smith has been fired."

Her eyes widen as she frowns "Why?"

I give her a look. "You know why."

She seems uneasy for a moment. "How did you manage to get him fired?"

"You know how we live in the Beaumont Building?"

She nods.

"Do you know who owns Star Gaming?"

She shrugs and says, "Dane Beaumont..." She trails off as a look of epiphany crosses her face. "Does he own this building too?"

"He does, and he's a friend of mine. He didn't like hearing about Bill Smith's actions, so he handled it. I just told him what was going on."

She frowns at me for a moment. "I don't need you to fight my battles but thank you." Her voice softens by the time she gets around to expressing her gratitude. "I'm glad he won't be able to do that again, but you really should have talked to me first."

I nod my agreement, though I don't reveal I have no regrets about handling it myself and presenting it as a done deal after the fact. I understand she doesn't want me treating her like a child who needs someone to think for her and handle her business, but she's my concern now, whether she wants to admit that or not. I have no intention of stepping into some kind of daddy role, but I also won't stand by and let her be hurt if I can stop it.

Chapter Ten

Keaton

AFTER OUR NIGHT TOGETHER, I at first feel a little shy around Evan. I immerse myself in the game I'm designing, which means confining myself to my room for hours at a time. I'm not sure if I'm hiding or just regrouping, but he's patient with that for at least a few days. It's day number four, and we've barely interacted since he told me about his interference in the Bill Smith situation. When he knocks firmly on my door, my brain is still entangled with code, so it takes me a moment to respond.

"Open the door, Keaton. You can't keep avoiding me." He sounds terse.

I blink, realizing he's taking my silence the wrong way. "Come in," I say loudly. I turn in my chair as he enters, once again reminded how devastatingly attractive he is, along with how tall, as he walks forward. He practically looms over me, and I shiver with anticipation and perhaps a touch of anxiety. I stare up at him, and his stern expression makes my mouth dry. I licked my lips. "Do you need something?"

"I'd like you to stop avoiding me. I thought you were okay with me dealing with the Smith situation. It feels like you're giving me the silent treatment."

My eyes widen as I quickly shake my head. "I'm not. I really do appreciate you interceding. It's just..." I trail off, drawing my lower lip between my teeth. How do I explain this? "I feel a little awkward around you." I blurt it out, and it hangs between us in a cloying fashion that makes me nauseated.

He frowns, but he doesn't laugh. I don't know why I expected him to, but all he does is sigh as he sits down on my bed, arranging himself so his knees are touching mine. He leans forward, taking my hands in his, and I grasp his fingers with my own. We stare at each other for a moment, and then he lets out a heavy sigh. "I don't want things to change between us, Keaton. I want you to feel comfortable here and with me. I don't regret the night we spent together, but it seems like you do. If you want, we can try to pretend like it never happened."

Since we already discarded that idea, I shake my head. "No, that isn't it. I don't want that at all. I just want to have a chance to adapt to everything, I guess." I shrug a shoulder as I squeeze my hands around his.

"It's one thing to have a silly fantasy, and quite another for it to become reality. I don't know where we're headed, and I guess I'm a little anxious about what will happen if things end badly, but that doesn't mean I want to turn away from you. I guess I've been terrible about hiding here in my room." I give him a bright smile, introducing a note of forced cheer. "On the plus side, I've finished three more levels."

His lips turn up into a small smile. "At least some good has come of it."

I nod, anxious to move past this blip. "That means I'll be out of your way sooner than expected, maybe." Assuming I can actually finish everything and make the game successful.

He scowls, which isn't the reaction I was hoping for. "I don't want you out of my hair. I want you to stay, Keaton. I know we've covered this, but I want to make sure I'm clear about it. Things are different with you than they've ever been with anyone else. I feel a lot more for you than I ever did in the past, and I'd hate for us to throw away what can make us happy."

I nod my agreement, wanting that, and he leans back. I feel bereft when he lets go of my hands and gets to his feet. "Where are you going?"

"I'll let you get back to work. Dinner will be ready in twenty minutes though, so it would be nice if you surface for that." He sounds good-humored, but there's a note of sincerity and perhaps a touch of pleading beneath his lighthearted words. How can I resist or refuse?

I pretend to consider the idea. "What are you making?"

"I'm making Vietnamese food magically appear from the takeout menu." He grins as he shares that.

"That sounds perfect. I'll have the eight." I stare after him for a long moment once he's gone, the door closed behind him. If my brain is cooperating, I can probably finish at least this section, but as I slowly turn back to my computer, I see his face instead of the coding, and despite my best efforts to get back into a working frame of mind, it's a lost cause. It isn't long before I push away from the desk and go to join him.

We sit in the living room to eat, and the conversation flows better than I'd hoped. I still feel a little stilted and shy around him, which is ridiculous considering everything we've shared so far, but he has a low-key way of putting me at ease. After our food is finished, he draws me back against him, puts his arm around my shoulders, and turns on a movie.

I lean against him, so wrapped up in his proximity that I miss the first half of the movie. Thankfully, it's one I've seen before, so I can bluff my way through. I suspect he's not paying any more attention to the movie than I am by the way his fingers continue to caress my shoulder, and by the way he periodically turns his head to nuzzle my cheek, but it gives us a good excuse to sit quietly and cuddle without the need for conversation, or the expectation that it will lead to sex. Not that I object when it inevitably does later in the evening.

THAT SETS THE TONE for us, and we spend the next two weeks getting used to each other. The awkwardness soon dissipates, and before I know it, I feel like I'm at home. It's not just with Evan, but also with his apartment, and even the city itself. It's so different from Michigan, but there's a vibrant energy in the city that never stops, and I already can't imagine returning to the town I left behind. I'm sure it would feel too small, like a tight wool sweater. I'd never be comfortable again.

Of course, if things don't work out with Evan, I'll probably end up there anyway. Maybe I'll appreciate having the smaller confines of our hometown to hide away and lick my wounds. I can't guarantee he's not going to break my heart, and part of me fears it. It's that part which has a hard time letting go and fully embracing how I'm starting to feel for him. I don't think I'm the only one with reservations, because he seems to be holding back somewhat as well.

He comes home a few days later, and he looks annoyed. I frown up at him from where I sit on the couch, laptop before me while I work on code. "Is something wrong?"

He shakes his head, but he still looks irritated. "Vanessa just told me about this business function we're expected to attend this weekend. Ostensibly, it's a cocktail party, but it's really just an excuse for networking. I hate these things, and Vanessa insists she had it put on my calendar weeks ago, though my assistant hasn't heard anything about it either." He runs a hand through his hair, disheveling the brown locks.

That makes my fingers itch to correct the disarray he's left behind, or perhaps sneak in a quick stroke. "I can't blame you. It sounds boring." I like parties as much as anyone, but real parties, not that stodgy business suit stuff he's talking about.

He brightens suddenly as he looks at me. "Why don't you come with me?"

I arch a brow. "I can't see why I would do that." Realizing I might have spoken too bluntly by the way he winces, I hurry to add, "It's not that I mind going with you. I just don't think I would fit in with your crowd, and I don't want to embarrass you."

He scowls. "You're never going to do that. Say you'll come, Keaton. I hate going to these things alone, and I really don't want to stand with Vanessa for two hours while I pretend to like a room full of people I have little use for beyond professionally. They're certainly not my first choice for socializing." His eyes gleam as he tacks on an alluring promise. "I'll buy you a new dress."

I frown, wanting to reject that idea, but the truth is, I certainly have no cocktail dresses in my wardrobe. It feels a little sleazy to be using money from him for a dress though, and I shake my head. "I can buy my own."

He moves closer, coming to sit beside me as he starts to undo his tie. "Really, I'd be happy to. You're doing me a favor, so why should you spend your money on something you'll probably never wear again, unless you go to another function with me?"

For a moment, my pride urges me to keep resisting, but he's speaking some truth. I'm unlikely to wear the dress again, and I truly can't afford something that costs hundreds of dollars since I'm trying to budget what I have remaining. Not having to pay rent has been a big help, but I absolutely refuse to ask Evan to buy my personal items.

"Keaton?"

I blink and look at him. "Well, okay. I still think you're going to regret this." I smile, but some of my anxiety must bleed through.

He lifts a hand and cups my cheek, rubbing his thumb down my cheekbone in a gentle fashion. "I'll never regret a chance to spend time with you."

With that in mind, I accept the credit card he gives me the next morning, prepared to find something suitable for the tedious event before us. I'm sure being with Evan won't be boring, but I can't muster any real enthusiasm for a business cocktail party. Still, it's fun to shop, and a brightly colored fuchsia gown catches my attention. It's not my usual style, and I decide maybe that's a good thing as I select the dress, sign the credit card receipt, and stuff it in the bag without looking. I'm almost afraid to know how much it costs.

Chapter Eleven

Evan

WHEN SHE ENTERS THE living room that Friday evening, she takes my breath away. The first thing I notice is a screaming fuchsia color, which seems a bit jarring and garish compared to what I'm used to seeing, but she makes it work. Her hair is rolled up in some kind of elegant configuration, and her makeup is perfectly applied.

I'm not used to seeing her wearing it, and it gives her a smoky, exotic allure, though I prefer her usual style. I know tonight when I kiss her, I'll likely taste that bright pink lipstick, and I almost grimace at the thought. Her natural lips are more appealing, but she's certainly striking this way.

She stands nervously in front of me after twirling, and I realize the silence has gone on too long when her expression starts to change from hopeful to concerned. I step forward, pulling her into my arms and pressing a kiss to her cheek to avoid smearing her lipstick. "You look stunning." She certainly does, though I wonder if she's going to like standing out among the crowd. Some women enjoy that kind of attention, but I don't know if Keaton will.

She seems bolstered when she steps back, and she no longer has that anxious look. I mean, she's obviously still a little anxious by the way she clutches my hand as we leave the apartment and enter the elevator, but she seems more assured. I guess it finally sinks in that she doesn't really have any experience in this kind of thing, and I show her a confident smile before noticing the woman sharing the elevator with us.

She stares at Keaton for a moment and smiles, and her friendly expression must put Keaton at ease. "You look lovely, miss," says the woman.

"Thanks," says Keaton with a slight flush.

I look at the woman, wondering why she looks familiar. "Do I know you? Do you live in the building?"

She laughs in a rueful fashion. "No, but I might as well. I'm Dane Beaumont's executive assistant."

I nod as she says it, realizing that's how I know her. I've seen her at Dane's apartment a few times. I feel sorry for her, because she's clearly working late on a Friday night. I often burn the candle at both ends, but I rarely make Haley stick around much past six, thinking one of us should have a life.

Abruptly, I realize I've spent more time away from the office than I usually have ever since Keaton came to stay with me. I'm arranging it so I'm out of the office at six o'clock sharp, and I'm probably doing just as much work as ever, but I'm finding a way to cram it into the daytime hours so that my evenings are free for her. It feels good, and my hand tightens around hers as the elevator stops on the main floor.

We wait for his assistant to exit. I can't remember if her name is Caitlin or Kathleen or something else. She nods to both of us and departs, and I offer my arm to Keaton as we follow. My driver's waiting, and he soon conveys us to the home of the business associate hosting the event. It's a nice building, roughly on par with the Beaumont Building, but I'm on edge because I can see Keaton is growing more nervous the closer we get to the penthouse apartment.

When we step out, she gasps slightly, her fingers tightening around my arm, and I wince at the way her nails dig in. She's obviously intimidated, so I touch her hand gently to get her attention. "You look marvelous, and you're going to be just fine. No one will take their eyes off you."

She frowns, and I realize I might have given her the wrong encouragement. I quickly added, "They'll be fascinated."

"I'd rather they not notice me at all." As though thinking of her dress, she tugs at the hem then. That's when I realize how short it is, at least when I don't account for the fringe, and a surge of possessiveness bores through me. It wants to tell her never mind, and we're going home so she can change. I don't want other men to see her like this, but I manage to tame the beast. It might be how I feel, but I'm too civilized to tell her that—and smart enough to realize she would probably rightfully crush my toes with her heels and walk away.

It's too late anyway, because I hear Vanessa's heels tapping on the floor as I catch sight of her hurrying toward us. At first, she's smiling, but when her gaze moves to Keaton on my arm, her expression chills, and her smile slides off her face as though it was melted. Her expression becomes arctic, and her tone is definitely chilly when she says, "I didn't know you were bringing your little houseguest this evening."

I frown at her. "I hardly need to inform you who I plan to bring to any function, Vanessa."

She blinks, and she looks hurt, though I don't know if she's truly injured by my words, or if she's being dramatic. "I'm your *partner*, Evan."

My eyes narrow at the way she says that, and I'm sure I'm not the only one picking up on a strange emphasis. Keaton stiffens beside me, sending a questioning look my way before glancing at Vanessa and looking away.

"Business partner," I say quickly. "It doesn't affect you who I bring as a date."

She's frowning openly now at Keaton as her sour disposition spills over to me. "It affects me if it causes gossip and loss of business."

I glare at her. "Fortunately, that won't happen."

She seems on the verge of arguing for a moment, but then she shrugs and turns away. "Enjoy your evening," she says as she looks back at us, and it's difficult to determine to whom she addresses the words. They have a slightly sarcastic edge, but that doesn't help me determine if they're for me or Keaton.

Once Vanessa is out of hearing range, I gently tug Keaton forward despite her resistance. "Ignore her. This will be fine."

She still seems apprehensive, and her smile is a little shaky, but at least she's wearing one. "I'm sure it will. I'd ask why Vanessa doesn't like me, but it's obvious."

I arch a brow. "It is?"

"How long has it been over between the two of you?"

I blink, almost missing a step. "Over? Are you implying she and I were once together?"

It's Keaton's turn to look surprised. "You weren't?"

I shake my head. "Absolutely not. Vanessa's good at business, with a sharp mind and the compassion of a shark. Those assets are valuable in a business partner, but we're far too incompatible to ever consider dating. Besides, I don't mix business and pleasure."

I suspect Vanessa would be all too happy to do so though, and it explains why she's been short with me lately, and why things have been tense in the office. I wonder if I'm going to have to break up the partnership.

It's not even because of Keaton, though a part of me wants to protect her from any of Vanessa's vitriol. Mostly, it's because I don't want to work with someone who has designs on me in that way, especially since I know how manipulative and focused Vanessa can be. It's helped us complete more than a few business deals, but I don't want to be the deal she's trying to close.

"Maybe I misunderstood then. She seemed like she didn't like me because she was jealous." Keaton looks away.

"I have a feeling you're right," I say as gently as possible while I take her hand in mine and squeeze lightly. "I don't know if it's for the reasons you assume, or because she's afraid of gossip and the impact it would have on business, but either way, she's being unfair."

Keaton's lips twitch slightly. "Absolutely. After all, most people wait to get to know me before they decide they don't like me."

I laugh even as I shake my head. "I can't imagine anyone not liking you."

She flushes again, and she seems genuinely amused and more relaxed than I've seen her all night as we enter the front door, which is standing open. "I assure you, a few people have disliked me before. My ex-boyfriend, Chase, wasn't too happy with me when I broke up with him and told him I was moving to New York in a few weeks."

"He must've liked you at some point." I say through gritted teeth, having to fight down the jealous urge to demand to know details of how involved she was with Chase. Was she in love with him? Was he in love with her?

It shouldn't matter to me, since it's in her past, and I'd feel offended if she got worked up over relationships I've had before her, but I can't deny there's a primitive part of me that can't stand the thought of another man having touched her before me. Even worse, what if she gave him the same kind of soft glances and gentle words that she gives me sometimes? Or the passionate moans and clenching of her pussy when I'm inside her?

I shake my head, trying to push away the green monster, and we're soon circulating. I don't know how it happens, but at one point, Keaton is separated from me. I pause on the fringes of the crowd to look for her, not immediately seeing her despite how her bright pink dress stands out.

Every other woman in the crowd is either wearing red or black, as though they received some sort of dress code in their invitation. I can see Keaton is self-conscious about it, and she keeps tugging at the dress. If I can find her, I'm going to suggest we leave early if she's as miserable as she seems.

Before I have a chance, Vanessa approaches, holding out a glass of champagne. "Looking for your girl?"

I frown at her. "Keaton's a woman." I take the champagne, but I don't sip it. I'm not in the mood for alcohol. I just want to find her.

"She's in the ladies' room. I'm sure she'll return to you soon enough. Doesn't she have a curfew you have to worry about?" She asks the question so sweetly, but she's glaring at me as she does.

I turn and face her, lowering my voice and making no attempt to change my tone from one of true anger. "Mind your own business and stop insulting Keaton. She's not a child like you're implying."

"She's fourteen years younger than you, and it's just unseemly." She scowls at me. "I've already heard whispers—"

"Twelve years, not fourteen, and I don't care what you've heard." I cut her off viciously, though my tone is still low. "I won't discuss her with you, and I don't want to hear another word about it." For a moment, I think about introducing the awkward topic of how she might want something more than a business association with me, but this isn't the time or place, and I'm certainly not coolheaded enough to conduct the conversation in a logical fashion.

Her lips tighten, and then she shrugs. "Fine, but don't say I didn't warn you."

"I never will," I assure her in a mocking tone. It makes her shoulders stiffen as she turns and marches away without another word. It's going to make things even tenser at the office, but I can't regret the angry exchange.

A few minutes later, I have cause to reconsider at least some of her claims when Jeffrey Hennings approaches. We've done business in the past, but I've never liked him. There's a sinister edge about him, and I've always felt like I should warn all the female employees in my company to hide if he's coming in for a meeting.

I have no better an impression tonight as he approaches, clapping me on the back while he holds a glass of something amber in his other hand. I assume it's cognac from the whiff I get from his breath. I start breathing shallowly as I ease back, wanting to put distance between us.

Jeffrey apparently has no concept of personal space when he's inebriated, because he just follows, leaning closer in a conspiratorial fashion. "Where'd you find that sweet young thing?"

I scowl at him. "I don't know what you mean."

He gives me a knowing wink and nudges me with his elbow. "Sure, you don't. I'm talking about that luscious little piece on your arm tonight. Somebody said her name was Kelly?"

I don't bother to correct him, not wanting him to know anything about Keaton—not even something as innocuous as her first name. "I think you've had too much to drink, Jeffrey."

He snorts. "No such thing, man. I just have a question for you."

"I'm happy to discuss business at any time," I say in a distant tone.

He's clearly too past sobriety to understand my delineation between personal and business conversation. "Are you about done with her? If not, does she have a sister?"

For a moment, my fingers twitch as they form into a fist at my side. I'm already pulling back my arm before I realize what I'm about to do, and I take a deep breath and breathe through the anger instead. "Sober up before you talk to me again." With those words, uncaring if I seem rude to him, or if I lose his business, I turn and walk away.

When I see Keaton coming out of the bathroom, her eyes are red. She's visibly upset, and I've had it with this whole evening. I approach her, putting my arm around her shoulders and trying not to feel offended when she pulls away a tad. "Are you ready to leave?"

She looks relieved as she nods. "I've been ready for the last two hours."

I look at the clock. "We've only been here for an hour."

"Exactly," she says with a shaky smile that doesn't reach her eyes. She's still rapidly blinking and seems on the verge of tears. I refuse to allow the jackals in this room to see her sadness, so I whisk her from the apartment without bothering to share partings with anyone. Worry about leaving a negative impression on my business contacts is the farthest priority down on my list right now. Keaton is number-one.

I soon have her in the elevator, and then back in the car. The driver takes us to the Beaumont Building, and she's mostly silent despite my attempts to draw her out. When we reach the apartment, I expect her to finally be ready to talk to me, but as I turn to her, she's turning away. "Would you unzip my dress? I'd like to take a bath." She sounds exhausted and frail.

I don't have it in me to push her for a more in-depth conversation. I just comply, efficiently pulling down the zipper and not making it a sensual event. It's obvious she's in no mood for seduction, and I just want to talk to her and find out what's bothering her. If a bath will give her a chance to calm down, I can certainly handle waiting a while.

After she disappears down the hall, I go into my study and pour myself two fingers of brandy. It's been that kind of evening, but I still sip it rather than toss it back. I don't want to risk having my thinking clouded, especially since I hope to have a meaningful conversation with Keaton.

As the minutes tick past, slowly becoming an hour, and then an hour-and-a-half, I wonder if we're going to have that conversation at all. I'm a little concerned about her, and I freely admit somewhat inpatient, as I set aside my now-empty glass and stand up, leaving my study a few minutes later.

I walk down the hall, looking into my bedroom. She's not there, so I expect to find her in the bath. I'm worried she might've fallen asleep in there, so I hurry in only to find the room is empty. I touch the tub, and it's completely dry, so unless she bothered to dry it off after she finished, she never used this bathroom.

I don't think she'd have any reason to go into any of the other guestrooms, so I walk down the hall to the room she's been using since she moved in. Officially anyway, though she's been sleeping in my bed for most of the last two weeks, and her cosmetics and toiletries, limited as they are, slowly migrated from that bathroom to mine.

I never thought to check if they were still on the counter, but I'm not terribly surprised when I ease open the door to her room and find her in her bed. She must've taken her bath in the guestroom and then laid down in here. I'm confused as to why, and there's a surge of hurt going through me as well.

Is she hiding away from me for some reason, or is she just upset in general? I'd like to wake her to find out, but she looks like sleep was hard-won. There are tear tracks on her face, and her hair is disheveled. I reach out to push it off her face, finding it damp, which is probably from her bath rather than sweat.

Impulsively, I start stripping off my clothes, laying the suit over a nearby chair once I'm down to my briefs. I walk around the bed and slide in behind her, pulling her into my arms. I hold my breath for a moment to see if she'll wake, but all she does is sigh and snuggle closer. At least in her sleep, she has no desire to escape me.

I fall asleep with anxious thoughts, my mind worrying at why she felt the need to sleep away from me tonight. I hold her as tightly against me as I dare even as I start to drift off, not wanting to let go of Keaton ever again.

Chapter Twelve

Keaton

I WAKE TO FIND FAMILIAR arms around me, and I snuggle closer with a soft sigh of contentment. This is starting to become my new normal, but I abruptly realize it shouldn't, at least this morning, because I deliberately fell asleep in my old room rather than in his. My eyes fly open, and I find he's awake, just staring at me. Perhaps it should be disquieting, but he seems puzzled and a little lost. I can see the hurt in his expression as well, and when he asks, "Why?" I don't need clarification.

I suppose I should wiggle away, but instead, I bring up a hand cup to his cheek. "I had doubts." It's as simple and as complicated as that.

He frowns. "What kind of doubts?"

"Doubts about how I could ever fit into your life, and how this could work for us. I'm not wired to be the wife of a businessperson. I don't know how to do parties and all the faux niceties. Everyone I met last night was fake, and I don't know if I can ever be like that. And my dress..." I trail off as I shudder, recalling just how out of place it was.

The day I selected it, I had thought it was fun and elegant at the same time, but now, it seems garish and childish. It's the kind of dress a teenager might wear to a junior prom, not a grown woman would select for a business cocktail party. I should've stuck with basic black, or perhaps a slightly daring red, but I'd had no idea. I know now, but I'm still embarrassed by the faux pas. I know it's just one of many I'll make over the years if our relationship deepens to become something more than what it is now.

"I don't know where this is coming from—"

"From looks and comments I overheard, and…" I trail off for a moment to nibble on my lower lip. "Your business partner."

He scowls, his lips compressed into a tight enough line that a bracket of white appears around them. "Whatever she said, you should just ignore."

"She followed me into the bathroom, and she pointed out my inadequacies. She's not wrong, Evan. I'm not the kind of woman who would be an asset to you."

"Maybe not in business, but life is about more than business." His hands moves to my arms, and he turns me over on my back before straddling me. "I don't care if you cost me every client I have, but you won't. If you really care about learning some of the etiquette, it's easy enough knowledge to acquire, but I have no interest in changing you. As for Vanessa, I'm starting to suspect there's more to her negativity than just worrying about the business."

"You mean like her attraction to you?" He looks so stunned I almost giggle. How can he be so oblivious? "I suspect that's part of it too, so it wasn't like her words devastated me. It's just, I guess she illustrated what I already knew—I don't fit in with your people."

"*You* are my people." He grasps my wrists in his, pinning them to either side of my head as he bends down. When his face is near mine, he speaks with a level of intensity that makes me simultaneously shudder and quiver with delight. "I'll always choose you."

I stare up at him, recognizing the declaration for what it is. We might not yet be at the stage of exchanging declarations of love, but he's telling me he wants more. He's prepared to make this a long-term situation, and I have no objection. I worry about my place in his world, but it's easy enough to set aside those thoughts as I lift my head so my lips touch his, and we melt into each other.

Chapter Thirteen

AFTER A BLAZING ARGUMENT with Vanessa on Monday, she chooses to cool off by taking over a campaign in Paris. I had originally planned to head it up, but I'm happy to let her do it. I don't want to travel away from Keaton for that long, and it'll give her a chance to gain perspective. I'm sure Vanessa believes me now after I assured her there is absolutely no chance of anything beyond a business partnership developing between us.

After our argument, I'm actually second-guessing that decision too, so I ask my personal attorney to start looking into the idea of splitting our company. Keaton provides a steady source of support, and she's happy to listen to me complain about Vanessa for part of one weekend afternoon before distracting me with seduction.

It's exactly the distraction I need, and we make love passionately before falling into a heap on the bed. I pull her closer, wanting her body against mine. She lays against me in a complacent ball, her cheek pressed to my chest. I'm content, and I sigh quietly.

"Are you all right?" she asks without lifting her head.

"Perfect," I say, meaning every word of it. I bend my head and brush a kiss to the top of hers. Her brown locks cling to the hair on my face, and I realize I'm starting to get a beard and mustache. I haven't paid much attention to that for the last few days, and my face feels rough. Imagining how I might've left red marks on her body, I pull back enough so that she can look up at me. "Did I hurt you?"

She frowns. "No. Everything was perfect."

I ruefully scratch my stubble. "I was afraid I might have given you whisker burn."

She smiles. "Maybe, but I like it. I hope you don't plan to shave. It gives you a roguish look I find very appealing."

From a business perspective, I should probably shave it off, but at her comments, I decided it can stay for a little while. "You think I'm roguish?"

She holds up a thumb and finger, separated about an inch apart. "At least somewhat."

I grin. "Don't rogues tend to pillage and plunder?"

She looks briefly intrigued. "Like a pirate?"

I shrug a shoulder, feeling silly even as I'm envisioning her as a busty wench I steal away to trap on my ship. Before the idea can fully take root or blossom into more, the doorbell rings.

She frowns. "Are you expecting someone?"

I shake my head. "No." It's a Saturday. I suppose it could be a delivery, but it's kind of late for that. A tad impatiently, I slide out of bed and put on a robe before hurrying to the door. I expect it will be someone I can deal with quickly, so I'm temporarily stunned when I see Meghan standing there on the other side.

She's grinning at me, and I swear I forget how words come together as my mouth gapes open like I'm an idiot. All I can think about is Keaton still in my room, and if Meghan looks the right direction over my shoulder, she might see her friend emerge from the master bedroom. That's not the way I want her to find out about us.

"You look stunned to see me." She's grinning.

"Uh huh."

She tilts her head, looking slightly more concerned than cheerful now. "Are you okay? Have I truly stunned you speechless?"

I clear my throat, realizing I need to act as naturally as possible as I step back to let her in. "Of course not. I just wasn't expecting you. Keaton never told me you were visiting." I can't imagine such a thing slipped her mind.

Meghan laughs, seemingly oblivious to my discomfort and racing thoughts. "Nah, I didn't tell her either. It's a surprise. Guess what?"

"What?" I hope I manage to summon some level of enthusiasm. I don't want Meghan to think she's not welcome, though I can't help wishing she weren't here under the circumstances. As I hear the door to my room start to open, I quickly move forward and sweep Meghan into a hug, turning her so her back is to the hallway.

My gaze locks with Keaton's, and she looks startled for a moment, and then panic kicks in, and she scurries down the hallway. I don't let go of Meghan until I see Keaton slip into her room. She closes the door quietly enough that it doesn't reach us, and I breathe a sigh of relief as I take a step back. "What?" I repeat.

She looks confused for a moment as she steps back. "Wow, you must've really missed me." She seems a little surprised, but mostly touched.

I feel a little guilty for misleading her, but then I realize I haven't entirely. After all, I did miss Meghan. I haven't seen her for a while, having been too busy to go back to Michigan. I feel a little dart of regret and guilt when I realize I didn't even attend her college graduation. That meant I wasn't at Keaton's either, and if I'd gone, I might've had some forewarning about what to expect from adult Keaton. Maybe, based on my attraction to her, I wouldn't have issued the invitation to let her live with me in New York, though that invitation was sort of compelled from me at Meghan's prompting.

"Anyway, Mom and Dad are here too. Mom had a headache, so they went to the hotel room to lie down, but I'm supposed to tell you we're meeting for dinner. They just want to eat at their hotel tonight, if you don't mind, since Mom didn't weather the travel well."

I wince on my mom's behalf, knowing how much she dislikes traveling by car due to car sickness. On the other hand, my father hates flying, so Mom compromises and endures car rides as much as possible. I can imagine how she's feeling after a multi-day car ride. "This is amazing. I had no idea you were coming. What a treat."

She beams. "Where's Keaton?"

"She's in the guestroom at the end of the hall."

"The farthest one from you, huh?" Meghan grins and nudges me on her way by. "I guess you didn't want her to cramp your style."

I heave a sigh of impatience. "Despite what you might believe, and like I've told Keaton, I'm not a man-whore."

She just grins at me, clearly disbelieving, as she waves and rushes down the hall. I almost feel offended that she's cutting short the visit with me so quickly, but I understand Keaton's her best friend.

They're in Keaton's room long enough for me to take a shower and dress, and I spend some time pacing in front of the wall of windows, waiting for them to emerge. They eventually do, and Keaton is still wearing a robe. She walks Meghan to the door, and Meghan calls a parting to me on her way out, along with a reminder to show up at the hotel restaurant at seven.

I lift my hand in acknowledgment, waiting until Keaton has closed and locked the door behind Meghan before I approach. It feels like it's been hours that we were separated, and I can't resist the compulsion to reach out and put my arm around her waist, drawing her against me before turning her into a full hug. I cling to her for a moment, and after a second, her arms lift to encompass me as well. When I finally manage to let go, I look down at her as we step back.

"What brought that on?" She looks vaguely alarmed.

"I guess I just missed you." And I realized how fragile this thing is. We put off telling my family, but it's obvious we can't do that anymore. If we do, it crosses the line from privacy into lying and hiding, and I refuse to do that.

She swallows, and there's apprehension in her gaze. "Does this mean we're over?"

I gasp, taking a step back. "What? No. Is that what you want?"

She shakes her head instantly, which provides a small measure of comfort. "It's not, I know we agreed not to tell your family, but things have changed. They're here now, so I think we either have to tell them or end this. I can't stand to lie to them or hide it so blatantly."

I release a sigh of relief. "I was actually feeling the same way. I don't expect they're going to like the news, but we need to tell them." For emphasis, I draw her back into my arms, pleased when she offers no resistance. "There's no way in hell I'm giving you up. I love you, Keaton."

I expect the words to be hard to say, especially since I've never spoken them to another woman, aside from my mom and sister, which is quite different. Instead, they tumble out easily, as though they've been waiting to spring from the tip of my tongue for weeks. Maybe they have, and it's nothing but a relief to have them out in the open. Even if she doesn't feel the same yet, I'm glad to have told her.

Her eyes widen, and she blinks rapidly for a moment before she smiles. "I love you too, Evan." She lifts her head, and I kiss her. We could get lost in that all day, but I know it's getting late, and she still needs to have time to get ready for dinner. I imagine we could both use some time to prepare ourselves for the coming revelation.

We sit down for a bit, discussing strategy, and decide we'll tell them after dinner has finished, since neither of us wants an ugly confrontation while we're still eating, and I'm bracing myself for it to go poorly. I just hope my family can eventually come around and accept that I love Keaton, and she loves me. I don't want to think what will happen if they don't, but I already know who my heart will choose if it comes down to it.

I hope Keaton feels the same, and I'm sad that I have any doubt about it after she's already said she loves me. I understand how hard it will be for her if we have to turn our backs on my family though, since they're the closest she has to any family left either, and Meghan is her best friend.

I pray it won't come to that, and I'm sure if it were any other woman twelve years younger than me, my parents might put up a little fuss and move on, but they're going to feel naturally protective of Keaton. They're probably going to think I took advantage of her. I don't want them to think badly of me, because I love them and I'm close to them despite the physical distance that's come between us in the last few years, but I also don't feel like I need to explain and justify how I feel about Keaton.

Chapter Fourteen

Keaton

WE ARRIVE ON TIME AT the restaurant, and his parents and Meghan are already seated. I'm happy to see them again, but there's still an icy ball of nerves lodged in my stomach that makes me feel queasy as I sit down after exchanging a hug with Lily and Everett. I'm trying to act naturally, because Meghan had already seemed a little concerned about me earlier.

I'd dismissed it as just being tired, but I think her BFF senses are tingling, and she knows something's up. She probably has no clue what, and I doubt her thoughts have ever led her to consider the possibility Evan and I are involved in a relationship.

The first part of dinner is mostly small talk and catching up, and Everett's clearly proud of Evan when I tell them about what a creeper Mr. Smith turned out to be, before revealing Evan handled it when Everett seems on the verge of getting to his feet and tracking down my old boss.

"Have you had any luck finding a new job?" asks Lily.

I exchange a small glance with Evan, who gives me a reassuring smile. "I've been focusing on my own game. Evan's been nice enough to let me stay at his place rent-free in exchange for a percentage of the profits if and when the game takes off."

Everett frowns. "You're taking advantage of your sister?"

Evan and I both cringe at the same time. "She's not my sister," says Evan.

At the same time, I say, "He's not taking advantage. Let's be honest. I'm mostly a charity case, because my game is probably not going to do very well, but he's giving me a chance to work on it without the pressure of a full-time job. I insisted he take a share of the proceeds."

"I think that's very kind of you," says Lily as she looks at her son with a misty expression. "You've grown into such a thoughtful man."

"I suppose there's nothing harmful about it if it's at your instigation," says Everett. He still shoots Evan a disapproving look, but I'm sure it's because he's feeling protective of me, not because he really believes Evan is trying to take financial advantage of me. A percentage of nothing is still nothing, and I've heard Everett more than once worry that Evan might have become so caught up in commercial success that he's not the same boy he used to be.

He is most emphatically not a boy, but as for the quality of his character, I see no difference between the man he is and the younger man I have known all these years, other than this man is mature and not self-absorbed. I can't stifle the compulsion to reach out and squeeze Evan's hand lightly, but I make it quick as I say to Everett, "You have no reason to fear. Evan's a good man."

It seems to satisfy his father, but when I look at Meghan, she's frowning at me before looking down where our hands briefly touched. I wonder if she's starting to realize there's more than just friendship between us, but I don't know how to bring up the topic right now. We're hoping we can suggest going back to their hotel room and share the news there.

Conversation moves on, and before I know it, we're about to order dessert. As the waiter approaches, I realize someone is following him, and I brace for impact as Vanessa approaches. "I thought she was in Paris," I say out of the corner of my mouth to Evan, who looks up at my words, and he grimaces at the sight.

She stands near the table, hovering with an air of expectation. "I happened to see you across the lobby, Evan. How unexpected." She turns to his parents. "Mr. and Mrs. Middleton, do you remember me?

I'm Evan's partner." She says that in a suggestive way that makes my hackles rise.

It's clear Everett has no memory of her, but Lily must, and she quickly summons a gracious smile, though I can see her lack of enthusiasm as she stands up and holds out a hand to Vanessa, short-circuiting what looked to be an impending hug from the other woman. I doubt their acquaintance is anywhere close to a hugging level. "How lovely to see you again, Vanessa. Will you join us?"

I hold my breath, hoping she'll say no, but of course, she doesn't. I'm sure she's here to cause trouble. She must have gotten the information of our location either from Evan's assistant or through more nefarious means. She seems like the type to track someone's cellphone.

No doubt, she's realized we haven't yet divulged the details of our relationship. I don't know if she knows how connected I am to their family, but she's probably intuitive enough to realize his parents might object to him dating someone twelve years younger even if she doesn't know I'm practically like their adopted daughter.

After she sits, she spends a few minutes schmoozing with his parents, coming across as charming and witty. I can see how she's successful in business, as I almost find her likable for a moment, though I know it's all a façade. There's probably a decent amount of goodness in her, but she's never bothered to show it to me, and this is all a fake display to lull us all into a sense of complacency.

It doesn't really work, because I'm nowhere near complacent. Under the table, my hand rests on Evan's thigh, and I can feel his tension as well. Briefly, I wonder if I should just blurt out the news before Vanessa has a chance, but it seems like a harsh way to do it. On the other hand, hearing from Vanessa that we're involved is going to hurt his parents and Meghan as well, so I open my mouth, struggling to find the right words.

"Mom, Dad, there's something we need to tell you."

My mouth drops open as Evan speaks the words. He moves his hand on the table slightly, and I lift mine from his thigh to bring it to the table and place over his. We grasp hands as we face his family, and I can feel Vanessa seething with resentment at having been denied the pleasure of outing our relationship.

"You're finally going to tell them?" She practically coos with delight, as though she's happy for us.

"Tell us what?" asks Everett with his brows in a severe line.

I glance at Lily, and it's obvious she's already figured it out. She seems to be struggling between anger and sadness. Finally, with a deep breath, I look at Meghan, and there's no doubting how she feels. She's wearing an expression of betrayal, and she shoves back from the table. "How could you, Evan? She's my best friend."

"It isn't like that," says Evan.

"You've taken advantage of her," says Everett with an air of finality, and his words eerily mirror his earlier ones, though in a completely different context.

Vanessa is clearly enjoying the show, and she grins with delight. I've had enough of her, and I say, "Why don't you leave? You've caused enough trouble."

She looks affronted for a moment, but then she shrugs. "Very well. I think you should know, Evan, that I've already begun the process of dissolving our company. I'm going to keep as many of the clients as I can, and with any luck, you'll end up destitute." She practically purrs with satisfaction as she shares the words.

It's almost funny that Evan's complete lack of response soon has her looking crushed. I imagine she expected him to beg and plead with her to stay, or to wallow in misery at the idea of losing his company, but he barely spares a glance for her, and he doesn't speak at all. His gaze is still on his parents, and I look away from her too, watching Meghan struggling with her purse, which is stuck through the whorls of the chair. I imagine she could ease it off quickly if she weren't in such a state.

"Meghan, please don't go," I say softly, trying to encourage her to calm down and listen.

She just glares at me. "How could you do this to me?"

I open my mouth, not sure how to defend myself, and then I wonder why I even feel the need to. "We're adults, and our relationship has nothing to do with you, Meghan."

Meghan laughs, but it has a harsh edge, and as she frees her purse by ripping the leather strap, she glares at both of us and rushes away.

Lily and Everett seem on the verge of following, and I stretch across the table to put my hand on Lily's. "Please don't leave until we've had a chance to talk to you."

Chapter Fifteen

Evan

I CAN FEEL MY PARENTS' initial resistance, and I'm half-surprised when they don't get to their feet and follow through with their intention of leaving behind Meghan. My dad is clearly enraged with me, and it hurts that he thinks I did something dishonorable. I guess viewed through their eyes, them casting me as the villain and seeing Keaton as the innocent I've corrupted is understandable.

It's not like that, but I can understand why they're feeling upset, and why my dad is sending me a death glare from across the table. I swallow a lump in my throat and struggle to remain calm. "I didn't intend to fall in love with Keaton."

My mother gasps softly at the words, and my dad's eyes widen. "In love? She's like your sister."

"She's not my sister," I say firmly.

"It's not like I grew up with him," says Keaton quickly. "Evan had already moved out when I moved in after my parents died. We've been friendly, but we've never been especially close. The age difference was one of the reasons, but it doesn't matter now. We're both grownups."

"You're just a young girl with her head being turned the wrong direction." Lily sounds saddened as she says that. "I can't believe you led her astray like this, Evan."

"It was both of us," says Keaton before I can defend myself. She clutches my hand tighter, and she seems openly defiant for a moment. "We love each other, and there's nothing you can do to change that."

I can see my parents aren't responding well to her anger, so I brush my thumb across her fingers until she quiets, and I clear my throat. "I know you don't approve, but I hope you'll listen and understand we tried to fight this, but we couldn't. I love Keaton, and she loves me. I have every intention of marrying her when she's ready."

Keaton gasps, which sidetracks me for a moment from my parents, and I look at her and nod confirmation. I don't tell her about the ring I bought last week that's hiding at the bottom of my underwear drawer at the moment. I wanted to tell my parents about us first, though I'd been putting off the idea. We'd tentatively talked about going home for Thanksgiving in a few weeks and telling them then, but now they know, and there's no reason to wait.

I wish I could share my intentions in a more romantic way, and I'll be sure to give her a real proposal to make up for it, but I think the only way my parents will accept it is if they realize we're not just indulging in a fling, and I'm certainly not seducing her for kicks.

"I just don't understand it. What could you two possibly have in common? Keaton, you're just beginning your life, and Evan, you're farther along in yours. You should be thinking about getting serious and settling down, while Keaton should still be out having fun." Mom seems genuinely puzzled.

Keaton frowns at my mom. "I had some fun in college, Lily, but you know me well enough to know that's never really been my scene. When I went to parties and out to do other things, it was usually at Meghan's behest. I'm just as happy to sit home playing a video game or designing my own game."

"I just don't want you to feel trapped and like you made a mistake, wasting your youth in a few years, Keaton." Lily shakes her head.

I frown at her. "You married Dad right out of college."

Mom flushes, and she quickly looks at Dad with a reassuring smile. "That was different. We were the same age, and we went through the same experiences together. I have no regrets."

"I guarantee you now, I won't either. It's twelve years. It doesn't really matter in the scheme of things, and if we don't care, why do you?" asks Keaton.

Mom stiffens at Keaton's words for a moment, and I think she might continue to argue, but after a second, a soft smile takes its place. "I suppose you could do much worse, since we tried to raise both of you to be kind, thoughtful, and considerate people. Of course, your parents had a huge impact on you being that way as well, Keaton."

I release a small sigh of relief as my mom reaches out and takes Keaton's hand, squeezing it lightly. I know we've won her over to our side, and with her support, hopefully, my dad will yield as well.

He still seems reluctant, and he says, "Since when do you have any interest in settling down, Evan? How is marrying someone and committing going to fit into your New York lifestyle? A different girl every week, and all your business dealings..." He trails off with a shake of his head.

I frown, starting to get an inkling of where Keaton and Meghan got the impression I'm a womanizer besides from just Ethan. "Dad, I hardly have a new woman each week. I've dated a few different people, but nothing serious or long-term, because I never had any interest in making it that way before. I can assure you, I'm not going to grow bored or restless, and I'm not going to change my mind. I love Keaton. That's something I've never had with any other woman in the past. The love was never there, so there was no motivation to change things or fit her into my life."

I maintain eye contact with my dad as I speak in an unwavering tone. I feel somewhat ridiculous trying to earn his approval at my age, but the circumstances are strange enough that I'm compelled to do so. It's not just me who will face the loss of family if they decide to cut us off. I don't want Keaton to go through that after losing her own parents. As much as I love her, I know I can't be all the family she needs.

It takes my dad a little while longer to come around, but by the time we finally end dinner, they both hug Keaton. Mom hugs me without any hesitation, and my dad follows suit, though his embrace isn't quite as tight as it was when we first hugged before dinner began. He still seems a little unsure, and he says quietly, "Don't break her heart. I don't want to be in a position where I have to choose one of you over the other, my boy."

I shake my head. "I'll never do that to you, and neither will Keaton. I just want you to keep an open mind and let us prove that to you."

My dad gives a grudging nod. "I guess you don't owe me anything anyway. I just want to look out for her since her folks aren't around to do the job."

I clap my dad on the shoulder as I step back. "I can't ever find fault with you wanting to protect Keaton. That's what I want to do too, Dad."

That more than anything seems to get through to him, and he hugs me once more. It's a regular hug, tightly clasped against him, and it feels like it's full of love and acceptance. My parents are clearly on board with the idea, at least enough not to protest and make us miserable, so now we just have to get Meghan to see things our way.

I worry about that. She can be just as stubborn as the rest of us.

Chapter Sixteen

THE MIDDLETONS ARE supposed to come for breakfast, and Lily and Everett show up at the Beaumont Building apartment on time, but Lily looks regretful. "I couldn't convince Meghan to come."

My heart sinks for a moment, and tears burn at the back of my eyes. I'm on the verge of crying when anger takes over. I love Meghan. She's like a sister to me, and I don't understand how she can't see this is hurting me too. "I'm going to see her," I say to Lily and Evan, who stands to the side of me.

He immediately pulls out his phone. "I'll call the driver."

After a moment, Lily reaches into her purse. "You'll need this." She holds a keycard. "We're all sharing suite three-twenty-four."

I take it with a nod, appreciating her removing that barrier, because Meghan can be mulish enough that she might not even open the door for me.

Moments later, I sit in the car as the driver takes me across the city, stewing in my own anxiety while alternating between anger at Meghan and understanding why she feels betrayed. I haven't actually done anything to betray her, but I did keep the changing relationship from her, along with my feelings.

I'm sure she guessed sometime in the past that I had a crush on her brother, but we never really discussed it, and I never admitted that it has become more. She probably assumed it had faded with time, just as I had until I returned to his proximity, and it flared to life again before maturing into something far more.

A half-hour later, I'm standing in front of the door to the suite. I think about knocking, but I doubt she'll even acknowledge it, so I just use the keycard to let myself in.

Meghan is in the living room area, and the TV is on, but she doesn't appear to be paying attention to it. Instead, she's looking at her phone, and she jumps with surprise when I say, "Hello, Meghan."

She glares up at me as she gets to her feet. "What are you doing here? How did you get in?"

I briefly lift the keycard and wave it before sliding it into my pocket. "Your mom gave me this."

Meghan scowls. "Great. Now she's betraying me too."

I could roll my eyes at her dramatics, but I'm here to make peace, not extend the war. "She's accepted that Evan and I love each other. I'm hoping you can do the same, Meghan. You're my sister in every way that counts, and I hate the thought of you being angry with me or turning away from us."

Meghan's hands go to her hips. "And I hate the idea of what you're doing with Evan. How long has this been going on? How long have you been lying to me and hiding it from me?" Her voice is thick with pain.

I flinch as I step closer, holding up my hands in what I hope is interpreted as a gesture of peace. "Too long," I admit. "We weren't sure how to tell you, or how you would react. We figured there was a possibility you might all disown us, so we put it off. I've been drawn to Evan for a long time, but it didn't become a relationship until I moved here. It happened within weeks, and you don't know how many times I wanted to tell you when we were talking on the phone or texting each other.

"There're so many pictures in my phone that I haven't been able to share because you would find them suspect. It's killing me not having you in the loop, Meghan." I don't bother to try to hide my pain. She needs to know I'm sincere. I have to get through to her if I want her to see I didn't set out to hurt her, and I didn't come to Manhattan with the scheme of seducing her brother.

"I don't like the lying. He hasn't done anything to you that was inappropriate, has he?" She seems ill as she makes the suggestion.

A surge of anger threatens to overtake me as I feel defensive on his behalf, so I take several deep breaths to keep from making an angry retort. "Of course not. He never even noticed me as a woman until recently. I've always been your best friend and the bratty younger kid. I swear, we were both adults before our relationship changed. Nothing sordid happened in the past. I love him, and he loves me."

I fully expect Meghan's anger to continue, so it's almost a surprise when she sits down and visibly seems to fizzle. "I don't like that you lied to me. You shouldn't have hidden it. I think that's what bothers me. It's not the idea of you being with him, though I don't want to hear anything about it in the future—"

I can't help a nervous giggle. "I promise, there will be no sex talk about your brother and me."

Meghan grimaces, clearly disgusted by the thought. I can't blame her, though part of me still giggles at her expression and reaction. I'm wise enough not to let it emerge as a sound though.

She sighs after a moment. "How serious is this thing?"

"You know how your parents joked about adopting me once, and we both loved the idea of really being sisters?" At her tentative nod, I smile and say, "This is as close as we're going to get. Evan proposed last night." I hold out my finger to show her the ring.

For a minute, I recall how he got down on his knee in the bedroom after fishing around in his sock drawer and made an official proposal. We had planned to tell his parents and Meghan this morning, but I'd been diverted from the task by my need to confront Meghan. I wonder if Evan has already told them, and I suspect he has. He was eager, and I doubt he's going to have the fortitude for a long engagement. Neither do I, for that matter.

Her eyes widen, and she stands up again as she walks over, lifting my hand to look at the ring in an appraising fashion. "It's a bit flashy for you, isn't it?"

I look down at the princess-cut diamond, which is bigger than I would usually select, but perhaps I'm just a besotted fool, because I love everything about it. "It's gorgeous. I never want to take it off."

Meghan snorts, but then she draws me in for a hug. "In that case, congratulations, sister." Having her arms around me feels like the best feeling in the world for a moment as I hug my best friend, happy she won't be trying to stand in the way of my relationship with Evan. I can't bear to lose her, and I can't live without Evan. Her making peace with our relationship is the best possible outcome.

Epilogue

Keaton

I WAS RIGHT WITH MY prediction that he wouldn't want to wait long, so Evan and I marry just six weeks later in a small ceremony in our hometown. While New York is our home now, it felt right to come back to the place where it all began.

It also gave me the opportunity to go by my parents' gravesite a couple of days ago. I'd spread out a blanket and told them everything, hoping they could somehow hear me. I'm sure they would've had reservations if they were still with me, but I know they'd want me to be happy, and I spent some time assuring them Evan does just that.

For a moment, I blink as I look around the reception, feeling the definite absence of my parents. As wonderful as Lily and Everett are, I can't help wishing Mom and Dad were here with us, and that it had been my mom who had helped me with the veil rather than Lily earlier in the day. Still, I'm luckier than some people, because I have this amazing family who took me in and made me part of it, and I'm officially a Middleton now.

With that reminder, I glance at the white-gold band nestled on my finger that matches the engagement ring that has rested there for the last six weeks. It sends a shiver of pleasure through me, and my gaze seeks out Evan, who stands across the room with his father. I start walking toward him, and as I get closer, I realize they're discussing business. I hover for a moment in the background, not wanting to interrupt.

"Did you find a way to deal with Vanessa?" asks Everett.

Evan nods, though he clearly doesn't want to discuss his ex-business partner. "She managed to snag a few clients, but I had enough advanced warning about her impending split to start doing some damage control of my own. The company is fine, and we'll rebuild our clientele. We have no worries, and I wouldn't be surprised if some of our former clients return after dealing with Vanessa. She was always good at schmoozing, but she wasn't so good at the substance behind the artifice."

"That's good, son."

As I approach, Evan and Everett turn to face me, and Everett smiles. "I think you owe me a dance, Keaton."

I can't argue with that, since it's about time for the father-daughter dance. The band must be paying attention, because they stop playing their current song and begin playing "Butterfly Kisses" instead. Tears immediately come to my eyes as I imagine it's my own father dancing with me when we take the floor.

Everett seems to realize, and he clears his throat. "I want you to know Howard would be really proud of you, Keaton. You've grown up to be a wonderful young woman, and he would be happy knowing you're happy. I feel confident saying he'd give you and Evan his blessing. So would Melissa."

"Eventually," I say with a small smile, trying to distract myself from the melancholy feelings trying to crash over me. This day has been full of bittersweet moments, but I'm glad I can still clearly recall my parents and imagine how it would be to have them here. Sometimes, I worry my memory is fading, but today, it's sharp and clear, almost like their ghostly presence is among us. I know they aren't, but I can feel them just the same.

"I'm very proud of you as well. I have to say, I think my son has excellent taste." He twirls me around for the rest of the song, looking teary-eyed himself by the end. He clears his throat as the music starts to fade. "I'm sorry. This is more emotional than I expected, and I guess I'll have to face it all again someday with Meghan."

I lean forward and kiss him on the cheek. "Thank you for always being there for me, Everett."

"Of course, sweetheart. You're like a daughter to me." He hugs me before handing me off to Evan, who's waiting patiently in the wings when a new song starts.

As my husband takes me into his arms, I curve against him and allow a few stray tears to leak out. He doesn't say anything. He seems to understand they're a combination of happiness and nostalgia. He just rubs my back for a moment until I lift my head, having regained control.

I look into his eyes, and I have no doubt Evan and I will going to be happy together. I'm sure Everett is right that my parents would give their blessing, and it adds an extra special touch to the day as I melt back into my new husband's arms and dreamily imagine the future before us.

About Kit

KIT KYNDALL IS THE pen name *USA Today* bestselling author Kit Tunstall when writing contemporary romance. It's simply a way to separate the myriad types of stories she writes so readers know what to expect with each "author."

Join Kit's Mailing List[1] **to keep up with her new releases across all pen names.**

---

1. http://eepurl.com/bpdvb9

Did you love *Out Of Bounds*? Then you should read *Reunion*[2] by Kit Kyndall!

"There will be separations, but there are always reunions."Ryder and Lisbeth were inseparable from kindergarten until they both decided to join the military. Ten years later, they're both back in Sage Valley. Lisbeth is home to stay, no longer wanting the structured life of service, while Ryder is benched from an injury that could end his career. With them both wanting different things, can the love they've always felt finally be enough to bring them together?

---

2. https://books2read.com/u/bQKXqd

3. https://books2read.com/u/bQKXqd

Also by Kit Kyndall

Kingwood Prep
Catching His Eye

Protectors
Safe Harbor
Hart & Soal

Pure Escapes
Ablaze
Out Of Bounds
Guarded
Succumb
Taking
Proposition
I'm No Saint Nick

Sage Valley
Reunion

A Second Chance

Seen
Catching His Eye, Part 1
Catching His Eye, Pt. 2
Catching His Eye, Pt. 3

SpicyShorts
Pawn
Two Cowboys for Cady
Ebony Enigma
Wrong Groom
Model Behavior
Biology Lessons
Mai Tais on the Beach
All Grown Up
SpicyShorts Bundle

Sweet Escapes
Falling For A Firefighter
Worth Waiting

Well...
Well-Seasoned

Standalone
Playing His Game
Snowbound
Student Bodies
Double Delights
Tied To You
Seduction
A Royal Pain
The Island
Submission
Falling For The Warrens
Billionaire's Baby Contract